The Way Around

The Way Around

Olivia Libowitz

Dedicated to Sophie Rubenson.
For the girl who always loved a good story,
this one is for you.

AUTHOR'S NOTE

This novel started in Paris. To be more precise, this entire concept was conceived between my entering the Louvre at ten a.m. on a Tuesday, and my departure not six hours later. The first sight I saw upon entering the lobby was a band of young children, all slumped together against a wall near the restrooms. They were dressed plainly, in jeans, white jackets, and solid colored T-shirts, with white tennis shoes. I had seen numerous "BEWARE OF PICKPOCKETS" signs that were scattered all across the city, and my mother and I had already caught several similarly dressed children in the act of brushing up against tourists near the Seine.

With these children in mind, I moved on to lunch at the Café Marly (located in the back of the Louvre, toward the Tuileries), my mother in tow. Once seated, I proceeded to spend the entirety of our meal making remarks such as, *"Gee, how cool were those pickpockets? Where do you think they live? What do you think they talk about? I wonder why there are so many more female pickpockets than males—do you think* Oliver *was just a lie?"*

God bless my mother for not smothering me with a croissant.

At the end of this book you will find a glossary of all the nautical and foreign words you might come across in this novel. You don't *have* to read it, but I do think it will clear up a thing or two for you.

This book means a whole lot to me. Read it kindly.

~Olivia Libowitz
Maryland
April 2014

"The sea, the great unifier, is man's only hope. Now, as never before, the old phrase has a literal meaning: we are all in the same boat."
—Jacques Yves Cousteau

Chapter One

There is nothing so disorienting as waking up in a place that is not the place where you fell asleep. For example: Say you were to fall asleep in a barrel sitting alone on a forgotten cart in the middle of a busy street, and you woke up some six or seven hours later below the decks of one of the king's merchant vessels, sailing swiftly out to sea. It is reasonable to assume that you would experience some level of distress and panic. However, panicking is perhaps not the wisest decision in that moment, because if you do happen to be tucked away on a ship that you have no business being on, in a barrel that you have no reasonable excuse for being in, then to be caught there would lead to a rather...hostile response from those around you.

This was the unfortunate situation that I found myself in upon waking from my completely accidental nap. You see, my first move once waking was to get my bearings about me, which was difficult seeing as I had absolutely no idea where I was. I didn't suffer this problem too long, for no sooner had I maneuvered one of my legs out of the barrel and onto the planks below, than was I charged from behind by a man shouting "What are you doin' aboard our *Dame Tromperie*?" He swiftly had my arms behind my back, and I watched in the bleary confusion of a recent awakening as two more men barreled down a set of wooden stairs at the other end of the room, assessed the situation, and came to help their friend drag me by my various limbs up the stairs and out into the open, at which point I was able to confirm my location on board a ship. How wonderful.

The three men were dragging me at an uncomfortably hasty pace, and my sea legs were at that moment so non-existent that I repeatedly lost my footing, my shoes slipping along the wet deck. The joints in my shoulders felt like they were popping out of their sockets, and I could feel my annoyance with the situation growing as each and every sailor we passed stopped his work to gawk at me as I was pulled along. After one particularly bad slip, my feet fell out from under me, and I grunted as my knees hit the hard wood below. The man who had found me growled to get up, and I glared at him.

"You know, if you weren't dragging me like a pack mule, I might have an easier time staying afoot," I snapped. "What are we rushing for anyway? Late for tea with Her Majesty, are we?" He yanked my arm again, forcing me to stand. Though he remained stony faced, I was sure I heard one of the two men behind me snort.

"Believe you me, boy, you won't be so funny after the Captain's done with you." He looked smug, and I could tell he was pleased with the threat. He leered down at me, a snaggled tooth catching on his lower lip. We reached the door of what appeared to be the main cabin. It was toward the bow of the ship, a large platform with three stairs leading up to it; a railing lined the edge of the platform. The door to the cabin was a deep red color, bordered with what appeared to be Celtic knots, and closed tightly.

Snaggle-tooth stepped forward and rapped sharply on the door, then stepped back. We waited for a moment as the sound of wood scraping across wood came from inside the room, and then the door swung open.

When I was younger, my brother had told me stories of fearless ship captains who faced off against ghastly ocean threats with nothing but their crews and their pistols. They were always described as tall, scarred and sea-weary, with thick skin and calloused hands, full of knowledge and wisdom that comes only from traversing the globe by way of the oceans. There had been a time in my life where I had wished to become a sailor. Despite my father's quick refusal of the notion, I had always admired the idea of captains.

The man before me, however, was quickly abolishing any and all heroic fantasies I had about such men. This captain was short and round like the baker who worked across from my house. He had a large beard, which was red and curved up around his ears, concealing half of his face. He was clearly young, most likely no older than my brother, who had only last year had his first child and reached the age of eligibility for King Louis's court. The captain's eyes were large and green, and he had a boyish hue to his cheeks, which made him appear almost younger. Despite his boyish air, his thick brow was heavily creased, and his lips curved downward in obvious distaste. He practically gave off waves of annoyance, and I could tell he wanted to see me about as much as I wanted to see him.

He glowered at me for a moment, before turning his head to the side and spitting over the railing. He licked his lips.

"Who's the shrimp, Octave?" he asked. Snaggle-tooth shook my arm roughly.

"Introduce yourself, boy."

I sniffed, the ocean spray hitting my face.

"Marin, sir."

"He's a stowaway, Captain."

I sneered at Octave. "I'm not a stowaway. I'm not supposed to be here; I don't even want to be here." I looked back to the captain. "Sir, if you please, my name is Marin L'Émule, and I truly had no intention of coming aboard your ship. You see, I was with my father, by the docks, but he was doing some business, and I was quite bored—it was a day's worth of negotiating he was doing, you see."

I continued to hold eye contact with the captain. He was still scowling, so I knew I didn't have him persuaded, but he also hadn't thrown me head first off the ship, so I took that as a good sign to continue.

"I happened upon several other boys who were lost for entertainment, and I know that perhaps hiding games are not the highest form of fun, but there was little else to do. I hid in a barrel, sir, just an old wooden barrel on a cart, which looked like it hadn't moved in years. But you see, I fell asleep. Not my fault even, not really; the other boys were just awful at seeking. I didn't know the barrel was going to be taken on your ship, and I didn't mean to drift off."

Octave snorted and rolled his eyes. "The boy falls asleep in a barrel; what's that say about him, Captain?"

"It says that I'm probably very good at hiding," I snapped.

"Must be a nice trait to have as a stowaway."

"I already told you, I'm *not* a stowaway!"

"That's enough!" the captain barked. I felt Octave tense next to me, his grip on my arm becoming painful. The captain peered at me hard. "It's a nice story, boy, without a doubt. But have you any proof of such a misunderstanding?"

I paused, shifting from foot to foot. What was he looking for? My father and I came from Paris by carriage; there was no proof of passage into the docks as he had only been coming to meet someone for supper and a discussion of business. I glanced at my clothes—surely this captain could tell I was no stowaway. I was dressed well; my hair was brushed this morning, though perhaps the barrel and the harsh ocean breeze had mussed it. There were no holes in my shirt or pants; my mother wouldn't have let me leave if there had been. I didn't look like any of the street dwellers who squatted on Lafayette, outside of my house. They were always dirty, with their heads tucked away to their chests.

I, on the other hand, looked—well, respectable. And why shouldn't I? My father taught men my brother's age, who were learning Latin and how to read the Holy Book. My mother taught as well, though she instructed girls younger than me how to read and sew. My brother was this year applying for a place in the King's scholarly court, and I would surely follow in his footsteps when I came of age. The idea of someone like me hiding away on a ship was preposterous. Surely no one needed to hide aboard a ship when he could pay his own way?

That was it! With a breath of relief I shoved my hand in my pocket and pulled out the small tin my father once kept for tobacco. When he had decided to throw it away, I asked him if I could have it instead and use it to hold my coins. In it I now kept eight sols, three silver écus, and my two precious golden Louis D'or. It was not enough to render anybody aboard the ship speechless, but it was a significant amount for a cutpurse to be able to get away with. I stuck it out toward the captain.

"Here then, if I'm your poor beggar boy, I must have some very favorable luck." I watched as he sifted a rough finger through the coins. After several moments of silence he snapped the tin closed and shoved it into the pocket of his brown jacket.

"Pardon me, *sir*, that's mine."

Octave growled, "You watch your mouth when you talk to Captain Dejafosse."

Dejafosse held out a hand for him to be still. "Now, now, Octave. It's his tin; let him have his temper." He smirked at me. "I'm afraid this is no short journey you're on, son. We've set a course for Pondicherry. Do you know where that is?"

I scowled at him. This man's patronizing tone made me bolder than I would have been otherwise.

"It's in India."

"That's right. That's a six-month trip, you understand?"

I folded my forearms across my chest. "I don't understand, actually. We surely can't be more than a few hours from shore. Just give me a cockboat and an ore. I'll get myself back to Calais all right."

"It would take you days."

"No rush."

"Good. In that case you won't mind joining us for a while." Dejafosse sighed and ran a thick hand through his beard. "See here, boy. If you are what you say, then I certainly won't be dropping a rich man's son off our ship to float home." He turned to the still open doorway of his cabin, reaching inside and pulling a small brass key off the wall.

"And if, by chance, you *are* a no-good sneakin' stowaway—well, then I suppose we'll keep you aboard to deal with properly when we make it to shore." He shut his cabin door behind him and stepped around Octave and me.

"Come on, Octave; bring him down to the hold. We'll put him with the others."

My head snapped up as Octave began to drag me behind the captain toward the stairs to the lower deck. "Put me with the others? What others?"

Octave grinned toothily, digging his nails into my arm. "You didn't really think you were the only no-good rat to try to slip aboard the Tromperie, did'ja?"

Chapter Two

The walk down to the hold was not a pleasant one. It wasn't difficult to notice that this ship was perhaps not the pride and joy of the royal navy. In fact, it looked in places as if it were barely being held together. The wooden beams that lined the ceiling were a moldy green color and had so many holes in them that it seemed their only use lay in housing the many spiders crawling above our heads.

Dejafosse walked briskly, in a clear rush to get me settled and return to his work. I was certain that my sudden appearance had taken him away from far more important matters, such as taking a pair of sheers to his tangled chin. Octave, on the other hand, loped behind his captain with a pleasant countenance, going so far as to hum some gravely out of key tune to himself, twined with intermittent bouts of sharp whistling. I supposed it wasn't every day that this man had the joy of inflicting undue punishment on children.

We reached a dank hallway, which smelled of fish and rot, tucked away into a far corner of the ship. Dejafosse stopped before a closed door, turning to me and locking both his hands behind his back.

"This is where you will stay. Inside you will find the spare cloths used for bedding on the ship. There should be enough between the three of you to keep the chill from getting to your bones. That reminds me—" He turned to Octave, snapping his thumb and forefinger together repeatedly. "We've got two brats in the hold, who are—"

"—Louis and Marie," Octave interrupted. "According to the boy."

"—Cutpurses." The captain finished tersely.

I snorted, quickly brushing a hand over my mouth to stifle it. Octave turned on me, shaking my arm. "Something funny, boy?"

I raised an eyebrow at the man, again twisting my arms across my front in an attempt to loosen his grip on me. "You must realize those aren't their *real* names, of course?"

He reeled back, eyeing me suspiciously. The captain stood to the side, looking entirely uninterested in his mate's confusion.

"How do you know their names, then? You met them, eh? You met them before?"

"I haven't done," I said defiantly. "But I scarcely believe the King and Queen are tucked away in your hold. Or do you suppose your stowaways have very loyal parents?" Octave flushed an unflattering shade of red. He opened his mouth as if to speak, but found himself cut off by the captain.

"I couldn't care less what the brats' names are," Dejafosse snarled. "All you need to know is that they'll be your cabin mates for the duration of the trip."

I gaped. "Like hell! I'm not sharing a blanket with a couple of beggars!"

"You will, and you'll not complain," the captain snapped. "You get it better than they do, anyway. Consider your petty tin of coins payment for my generosity. You may leave the hold three times a day, to join the men for meals. You will be provided one pair of spare trousers, one spare shirt, and a pair of woolen socks; it will get quite cold in the evenings."

I felt my shoulders sinking, and a glance at Octave showed a look of shock on his face as well. Was it possible he actually felt a twinge of pity for me?

"Captain, you won't really be givin' our good clothes to some no good rat, will ya'?"

Of course not.

Dejafosse ignored him. "Don't give me that look, boy. You're luckier than the two in there; they're stuck in the hold day and night. They get their meals brought to them. You'll be lucky enough to smell the ocean and see the sun three times a day, but if you continue to annoy me you'll find those blessings taken back as well. Octave, let him go."

Octave released me reluctantly, and I rolled my arm out to rid it of the ache. I watched with disdain and trepidation as Dejafosse pulled the brass key once more from inside his breast pocket and inserted it into the keyhole of the door. The click of the lock sounded thunderous in the empty hall, and I held my breath as the door creaked open. I was nervous, though about what I wasn't sure. Octave pushed me in roughly.

"Well, then, meet your new bedmates. We'll be back for you at meal time, boy." With that, I was thrust into the room, and into a world I wasn't certain I was ready to face.

Chapter Three

The door slammed shut behind me, and I heard the scrape of it being locked, trapping me inside. I blinked as my eyes adjusted to the dim light of the room. It was mostly empty, as if it had merely been the place where the spare odds and ends had been tossed when preparing the ship. Two stacks of hay sat in the left corner, covered in several white cloths draped messily. To the right of the room was a desk, old and battered, with a drawer in the front and no chair in sight to sit upon. A basin sat in the corner directly to my right, no doubt used for…relieving oneself. I had the sinking feeling that this basin, like the rest of the ship, would remain unattended for much longer than was strictly hygienic. Next to me, on either side of the doorway, were two candlesticks, latched to the wall, lit and illuminating the room enough to see the final pieces of decoration: two thin figures pressed close together against the back wall.

"Louis and Marie" looked to me as any ordinary street rats should look. They were both slumped low to the ground, backs pinned to the cabin wall and hunched over slightly, as if to make themselves appear smaller. "Marie" sat with both her knees pulled up to her body, her ankles raised, as if ready to run at any moment (which, considering their occupation, might be the case.) From the looks of them, they were around my age—perhaps younger even by a year or so, maybe twelve years. The clothes they wore seemed nothing more than rags, and yet their garments gave the odd impression of being the remains of clothing that at one point may have been very nice.

"Louis" was wearing what appeared to be the tattered remnants of a general's coat, with six brass buttons lining the front, and red and white stripes across the bust. It was hanging open atop a brown blouse that might have once been white, and a pair of dark trousers tucked into leather boots, which must have had no less than six holes in each shoe. His brown hair was a thick mess of curls, hidden partially by a white band, which ran across his forehead and tied in the back of his skull. He looked a bit like a small boy who had tried to play dress up with his father's clothing.

Marie, on the other hand, seemed utterly uninterested in her appearance. She was covered from her shoulders to her knees in a dark blue nightgown, tied tight at her waist with a red sash. Her shins were covered in thin stockings, one brown and pulled tight up to her knee, the other green and sagging around the top of her black boots.

I wasn't particularly impressed with the both of them. They didn't seem to me to be proper thieves; no scars or eye patches or anything you might expect to see on dangerous criminals who lived on the street.

On the other hand, neither of them seemed particularly impressed with me, either. Louis' eyes were skimming me slowly, his brow creased in clear distrust. With his right hand he clutched Marie's fingers tightly, and his left hand rested lazily on his raised knee, the white string of a brown bandalore twined around his index finger. I watched as the wooden toy dipped toward the floor, nearly colliding with it, before Louis twitched his wrist and the trinket came climbing up the string again, back to its' owner's hand.

The weight of the silence pressed in on me. I brought my hand to my suddenly sore throat and rubbed it absently. One of Marie's eyes was hidden behind a veil of tangled brown hair, and the one visible eye was unnervingly fixed upon me. I cleared my throat.

"I never can shut up at church." They gave no reaction, other than a raised eyebrow from Louis. I chuckled sheepishly. "That means nothing, sorry. I meant that it figures I'd talk first, then." The girl leaned closer toward the boy and buried her face in his shoulder. "I don't suppose either of you talk then? That is, I'm sure you have the ability—or maybe not, I don't really know—but you don't want to talk, then? Will this be a permanent expectation? Not to say I don't like the sound of my own voice, but six months of it might become a bit much even for me—"

"Shut up."

I froze at the sound of the boy's voice. The bandalore came to a sudden stop as he grabbed it in his palm. I swallowed.

"Ah, then you do talk. Brilliant."

"I said shut up." He arched his back, a quiet pop resounding through the room as he cracked his spine. "Your pointless drivel is upsetting my sister, so if you have nothing of value to say, say nothing."

I felt my eyebrows shoot up as I looked at him. He had a dull look in his eyes, as if he had completely resigned himself to captivity. He reminded me of a cat I had once, when I was younger. We had found it on the street, thin and shaking. I begged my mother until she took him in, giving him food and a blanket to sleep on. However, instead of rejoicing in its new life, the cat spent his every waking hour sitting at the window, staring gloomily out at the starving cats still on the street, as if he wanted nothing more than to be rid of his nice, warm home and rejoin his brethren in the cold.

It was odd, I thought then, to feel trapped by luxury.

Of course, the ship *Tromperie* was not exactly a grand palace, but the hold was warm in a humid way, and these two were promised meals each day, and I believed this life had to be better than fighting for scraps on the street. Still, poor and cold or fat and rich, I wasn't about to let someone speak to me as if I were no more than a footman.

"I'll thank you very much to keep your opinions to yourself, *your majesty*." His eyes widened slightly in surprise, and the girl lifted her head off his shoulder. "I'm sorry your sister seems so easily rattled, but my pointless drivel isn't going anywhere. I suggest you get use to it."

There was a moment of tense silence, before the *whoosh* of the bandalore falling sounded again in the quiet room. "Louis" tilted his head back against the wall, staring at me down the bridge of his nose.

"What are your names, then? Because I'd bet my bed they aren't 'Marie and Louis'. Do you think these people are stupid?"

"They believed it," he replied loftily.

I rolled my eyes, moving over to the bales of hay and sitting down heavily on one of them. I shrugged my thick jacket off my shoulders, bundling it up and shoving it by my feet. "Trust me, I'm smarter than the lot of them."

"You're cocky."

"I'm Marin, and you are?"

He sat still for another moment before his sister tugged on his shoulder. He looked at her hard for several seconds before groaning quietly and shooting a murderous look at me.

"I'm Sacha," he muttered, sucking the inside of his cheek. He looked back at his sister who continued to watch him. "It was your bloody idea; introduce yourself, then. I don't care if he knows your name or not."

The girl pulled her knees tighter to herself, glancing at me warily. I sighed, putting my hands up in defeat.

"I get it, all right? You're a lady, and you're shy and what not. Plus, you're his sister, and he sticks up for you, and I'm just some no good stranger who's interrupting your sibling prison sentence or what have you. But look, you're stuck with me. This is six months; if you think you can get through it without saying anything to me, you're wrong." I smiled, holding out a hand in offering.

"So, let's try this once more, yes? I'm Marin L'Émule. And you are?" I watched as she leaned forward slowly and grasped my hand in her bony fingers. I started slightly as her face split slowly into a large grin, her eyes creased warmly. Finally! Perhaps this trip could at least be spent with enjoyable company.

"My name is Orpheline, and if you continue to pester my brother and me, I will pull your teeth out one by one as you sleep."

Or perhaps not.

Chapter Four

The first morning on board the Tromperie came as a relief and a disappointment. On the one hand, I awoke to discover that the whole situation had not been a mere nightmare, and that I truly was stuck inside the hold of a rotting ship with two fledgling criminals; however, to my distinct joy, I also noticed that I was still in possession of my various limbs, all teeth included, and that Sacha and Orpheline remained on their respective side of the room.

It took me a moment to clear my brain of the early morning fog, but the second I did I realized what had roused me.

A loud clanging noise was coming from directly outside of the door. A glance at the far side of the room found the siblings sitting up, bleary eyed and staring at the door with distaste, as if it had personally insulted them. A shout sounded through the wall.

"Oy, boy—get up. You have an hour to eat and not a second longer; it's your own fault if you waste it." Octave, wonderful. Just the man I wanted to hear first thing after waking. He sounded even more agitated this morning than he had last night, and I assumed he had been ordered to come and fetch me.

I pushed myself slowly to my feet as the door banged open. Octave stood, hunched over slightly, a thick rope flung over one of his shoulders. I raised an eyebrow, reaching down to snatch my jacket off the floor.

"What's that for? You're not planning on tying me up, are you?"

He huffed, although the look on his face said that if he had his way, he would be doing just that. "No, although it would do you some good. I've stopped my work to bring you up for your morning meal, so here's the deal; you're going to help me finish up top, and then, if you're good about it, I might feed you."

I stared at him incredulously. "So, my side of that deal is just getting the food I was already promised?"

"Exactly. Now shut it, and let's go." He stepped into the room quickly and grabbed my shoulder, steering me toward the door. I could have sworn I heard Orpheline snicker as I was pulled out.

He locked the hold door as I tugged on my jacket. He stuck the key in the pocket of his cotton pants and brushed past me, heading toward the stairs. He was a good deal taller than me, and even at his slow pace I had to hurry to keep up with his large stride.

"Aren't you supposed to feed those two?" I asked as we climbed to the top deck. He glanced back at me.

"It's not my job to feed 'em. Some other lad will take down some salt pork and biscuits later."

"Why don't you feed them? It's your job to feed me. Or am I just special?"

He rounded on me, jabbing a thick finger into my chest. "Now you listen here, boy; I do not feed you. I fetch you. I give you work so you can earn your miserable keep. Once I finish with you you'll go down and get your food from the galley like every other wretch on here. I have better things to do than feed you." He twisted his dirty hand in the clean white fabric of my shirt. "I may not have my clothes cleaned by mummy, or a pretty tin o' coins in my pocket, but rest assured that I get more respect from these men in a day than you'll get in your whole life. Do I make myself clear?"

His face was close enough to mine that I could smell his sour breath, and his eyes were too near for me to look away. I pinched my lips together for a moment, before nodding.

"Yes, sir."

He pulled back. "Good. Now, you know how to tie a knot? We're finishing up the rigging. Métivier started it earlier, but Lord knows he's useless at everything, poor fool."

**

It took Octave and me almost an hour to finish the rigging, during which time I found myself eagerly taking in the ship around me. Despite my extreme desire to be back at home in my own bed, I had to admit my wonder at the sheer size of the ocean we were sailing upon.

Every direction I looked, I could see nothing but the sea, stretching out and fading into black in the distance. In spite of her tremulous build, the *Tromperie* felt powerful atop the water, like some animal built of strong bone and sinew tearing effortlessly through the waves that crashed against her body. I sat in the crow's nest, high above the rest of ship, and stared out for a moment through the billowing sails. The edge of the ocean seemed a world away, and it both thrilled and terrified me to realize that there was even more beyond that; that I was sitting atop the planks of the only salvation around for months, and that I was condemned to stay here. Inside my mind, where I would have expected to feel fear, or possibly frustration at my fate, I instead felt some faint excitement, some tremble of satisfaction.

Once the last rope had been securely fastened to its peg, I hustled down the nets to the deck, where Octave stood waiting, leaning against the banister at the edge of the ship. He looked at me oddly.

"You have a question for me, boy?"

I shook my head. "No, sir, I've finished."

"Have you now?" He glanced up at the tied off ropes above our heads, unmoving. Finally, he sniffed loudly through his nose and looked back at me. "So you have. And you weren't up there ten minutes, were you…"

"Perhaps I'm a natural," I said, proud of myself.

"Perhaps next time you won't make it look like a chimpanzee had tied them off."

"Excuse me!" I cried indignantly. "They're secure, they are!"

"That may be," Octave said, peering at me over the bridge of his nose. "But this ship is a representative of the good king, and will therefore be kept up to shape. I figure a ponce-y thing like you would understand the appeal of looking presentable."

Moving toward me he gripped my arm once more, turning me toward the stern of the ship. I rolled my shoulder, shrugging out of his grasp as we made our way through the main door and into the galley. He grabbed me again, roughly.

"You know, you don't have to hold me every time we move. I'm not actually planning on making a run for it. Don't know where I'd go, do you?" His mouth twitched a bit, and I grinned. "However, if you *do* know a good way off this ship and back home that doesn't involve me returning in a box, I'm all ears."

"Would you mind returning in a barrel?" he asked. I snorted.

"Well, if that's the best idea you've got, maybe I'll stick around. I've heard those things are quite uncomfortable."

He looked at me, schooling his features into his usual scowl, before sighing slightly and removing his hand slowly from my arm.

I flexed my arm to regain feeling in my fingers. "Why don't you make the other two stowaways work? I would think you'd love to watch them break their backs for your men."

"You'd think that," he said, scowling and puckering his lips as if he were tasting something bitter. "Wouldn't work, we don't think."

"How do you know?" I asked.

He snorted. "The boy is no good to us; he'll only work if his sister works."

"And how do you know she won't work?"

"We let her go for half a minute so she could speak to the captain, and she kicked me in the shin and hollered more curses in one sentence than most of our men say in a year. If we let her go long enough to work, I can only assume she'd jump overboard and try to swim back to France."

I would have liked to ask more, but it was then that we reached our destination. As we turned the corner I was bombarded with the smell of roasted pig and fish. The galley was about as far from the hold as you could get. It was, in fact, a room that seemed to me upon entering to be extremely pleasant. The far half of the room was filled wall to wall with bronze cooking tools, pots and pans of different sizes and levels of distress; in the center of the room stood a large cast iron cauldron, within which there seemed to be some thick red soup bubbling.

The cook was strangely thin for a man in his line of work, but so tall and long-limbed that he somehow managed to fill up the whole space, with one arm to his right shaking a pan over a low flame, and the other arm stretched out to his left, sprinkling salt through his bony fingers onto some unidentifiable meat. His face was pale and his cheekbones jutted out, but his eyes were content, even though he had to crane his neck awkwardly to avoid hitting his head on the low ceiling. His legs were strange to look at, in that one was considerably longer than the other. His left leg came down to his mid-calf, and stood upon a wooden stilt strapped to his thigh. I at first perceived him to be an amputee, but a second look showed that he did in fact have a foot connected to the leg, it just decided against reaching the floor.

There were five other men sitting close together around a table a few feet in front of me, which took up most of the room. They were all dirty and tired looking, but grinning and laughing loudly. There was one older man with dark skin and bountiful wrinkles who was pounding his fist onto the table with mirth. They paused as we walked in.

"Well, my stars. Is that the fancy boy? Look at his nice shirt!" one of the men exclaimed, peering forward and resting his chin on his hands. The other men laughed.

A grey-haired man shoved his neighbor over. "Budge up then, son, make room for his majesty, the queen." He made a sweeping motion toward the now empty seat, and I felt my face heat up as the sailors continued to guffaw. Octave chuckled, shoving me forward.

"Go on then, Marin, eat with the big boys."

I sat down gingerly at the table, muttering a quiet "thank you" as the cook dropped a plate of pork in front of me. I glanced up and found the men staring at me, grinning. I flushed.

"What is it?"

A young man, probably only a few years older than me, shook his head, still smiling. "You been doin' the riggin', I hear. How was that? Scared of the heights, I bet."

I opened my mouth to defend myself, but Octave beat me to it. "Oy, watch yourself now, Métivier; the boy's quicker than you in the rigs, and he don't spill his guts over the side of the boat nearly as much, either."

I smiled nervously as the other men began to cackle again. The older man reached over, slapping Métivier on the back. He turned to me. "The name's Deole." He spoke in a thick island accent I had heard only once before, in the voice of a maid from Barbados who worked in my house. He was grinning, the wrinkles on his face becoming even more pronounced. "Then yuh had fun, did yuh?"

I nodded. "I didn't know a ship could be so grand!" I caught Octave's eye and paused. He smirked, raising an eyebrow. I quickly looked back to my plate. "What I mean to say is—well, it wasn't that interesting, I mean, it's just a giant block of wood with some ropes on it. I didn't do much anyway—I only tied up the sails, and it's not as if it was hard or anything, I suppose it doesn't take much wit to be a sailor—" I stopped as the men looked at me incredulously. "No offense intended, of course—but I guess it does what it needs to do as a ship. I've seen better, and it's not as though I wouldn't leave in a heartbeat if I could but I…um…" I trailed off, wincing. The rest of the men sat in silence for a moment, and in an attempt to stop my babbling I shoved the pork into my mouth and gagged, not prepared for the amount of salt on the meat.

Then they were laughing again. Even the cook joined in, pausing his ministrations. Métivier took his turn to pound his fist against my back as I choked on the pork. Octave stood, still smirking, against the doorframe, watching the other men with amusement. The sailor across from me reached over, gripping my shoulder and grinning.

"The lad has got it all right! Got the bug, and it only took some time in the nest." He ducked his head as he continued to laugh. I had, by this point I'm sure, turned bright red.

"What have I got, then?" I demanded, annoyed at the joke at my expense, which I did not understand. The men shook their heads some more and Deole let out a sigh, sharing a look with Octave.

"Aye, matey, we might get a sailor outta this one yet."

Chapter Five

For the next two weeks, I went about my day with a consistent routine: Each morning, Octave would come down to the hold to wake me and take me up top, where he would give me a task which needed finishing. The second day aboard he showed me how to properly mend a fishing net; the day after that I learned how to fasten supports to the mast; each day a new task was added which we completed before we ate our morning meals. It was always something trivial and finished quickly.

The first meal of the day was eaten hastily and with little talk, due to the fact that neither I, nor apparently Octave, were very good with mornings. On the third day I noticed that there were never the same men eating breakfast when I came in, but rather new men who I hadn't seen yet. Octave told me that the sailors worked in shifts, where each man had a set of tasks for each day of the week. On any given day a man might have three tasks, say cleaning, mending, and fixing—in that order. If fixing were to take him two hours longer than his other tasks, then he would most likely be very late for dinner, and late to bed that night. However, the next day he might be fixing, cleaning, and *then* mending. If that were the case then he would be very busy in the morning, and miss breakfast, even though he had eaten early the day before. Every man on board had a specific set of skills, and his tasks were mandated based on those skills.

It all seemed a bit complicated to me. I couldn't understand why they didn't just do the same tasks in the same order every day, but Octave said it made sense. I was apparently just too stupid to comprehend the workings of a mighty vessel such as the *Tromperie.*

I asked him what his skill set was, and why had he been let aboard the ship.

He told me to choke on a squid and dragged me back down to the hold halfway through my lunch. I learned not to ask him questions about his life.

Being on deck during the day wasn't bad; it was almost enjoyable, really. The sailors were friendly enough, despite suspecting me of being a stowaway. In fact, some of the men seemed to find it humorous that three street rats had gotten aboard the ship unseen. Supposedly, Captain Dejafosse was known for being the toughest captain in the king's line of merchant ships. They said he would have been in the armada, but he was too loose with his gun. I didn't find this as funny as the men did.

They also didn't seem to mind having me under foot. Octave had taken to assigning me tasks that nobody else on the ship wanted to do. I didn't mind; Dejafosse made rounds during the day and observed the men at work. The unappealing—and occasionally revolting—tasks I was assigned (scraping the barnacles off the ship's outer wall, emptying chamber pots, removing the droppings from the goat pens) were generally out of the way, and therefore allowed me to go several days without running into the captain.

Once my daily chores and meal were over, however, my life sailed into thoroughly unpleasant territory. I found that Sacha and Orpheline were not the type to warm up to strangers with time. In fact, if anything, they seemed to draw further into themselves and each other every day, whispering quietly with their backs against the far wall, and their distrusting gazes flickering over to me from time to time, as if I might pounce on them at any moment.

For the first week I had endured the silence with relative ease; the one conversation I had had with them consisting mostly of bodily threats and leaving me with the distinct feeling that I didn't really want to know people such as these two. However, as the second week began I found it increasingly frustrating to spend the majority of my day locked away in a dank room with no sound but the waves and the whispers crashing against the walls. It was my pride more than anything that finally prompted me to speak to them. I was not used to being ignored by youths my own age. In fact, there was not one child in my classes in Paris whom I had never spoken to, considering myself as kind as anyone else, as smart, as well spoken—perhaps I was short of temper in some moments and shorter of patience in others, but that had never warranted such ill-trust and unprompted dislike from others.

With all this in mind, I resolved myself to breaking the silence once and for all, and being able to spend the remainder of the trip in, at the very least, an amiable way. And so I made a plan.

On the first day of the third week, we woke to a light rain shower. I went with Octave for breakfast as usual, finishing the morning's riggings with as much speed as I could muster while trying not to get tangled in fishing wires. As usual, we then moved to the galley, and I sat at the table, spreading a napkin over my lap—an action far too sophisticated for the company, which warranted several hisses of "nancy boy" in my direction. I ate quiet and quick, while the men spoke around me about the chances of sea storms this time of year, as we headed around the coast of Africa. I paid little attention to the conversation, my eyes flitting between the men and the remaining scraps of food on the table.

It took ten minutes for the right opportunity to arise. The captain came sauntering down the stairs, his beard and hair wet from the rain. I greeted him with a quick "Captain", then waited until he turned his back on me; the other sailors—Octave included—standing straight at attention. As he reached out to check the fastenings on Deole's coat, I slid my hand quickly along the table, pinching the rim of a plate holding several biscuits and three slices of salted pork. I tugged it to me quickly, the contents of the plate spilling onto my lap and into the napkin. I tied it, and tucked it into the inner pocket of my jacket, pushing the plate back into place and standing. Dejafosse glanced at me.

"Did you need something, boy?" he asked. I shook my head.

"No, sir, did you?"

"Is that disrespect, L'Émule, or am I imagining that tone?"

I was, in that moment, uncomfortably reminded of my father. "No disrespect, just if you're done with me for the morning, then I'd like to get back to my room." That lie sounded terrible, even to my ears. Octave rolled his eyes behind the captain.

"Is that so?" Dejafosse asked, scowling. "And what, may I ask, is so important in the hold that you'd be anxious to get back to?"

I paused, picking my words carefully. "The wind," I said. "Last night the wind was creaking the walls so badly I couldn't sleep, but it's calmed down a bit this morning, I'd like to give it another try."

Octave snorted. "I thought you were good at falling asleep even under the worst conditions."

I glared at him. "Well, perhaps this ship is worse than the worst conditions, yeah?"

"That's enough!" Dejafosse snapped. "Very well boy, you want your sleep, go get it. And to ensure that you're well rested, why don't you just stay down there for the rest of the day. We won't interrupt your slumber until tomorrow morning, but only because we're so incredibly generous."

I groaned quietly as Dejafosse nodded at Octave, who stepped forward quickly, grabbing my arm and tugging me up the stairs and across the deck.

We passed the entrance to the hold and moved forward to the stern of the ship. I looked at Octave incredulously.

"Eh, you'll excuse me, won't you, sir, if I point out that you seem to have forgotten the layout of your ship? The hold was back ther—Gah!" I flailed as my head was suddenly dunked into one of the water troughs at the stern of the ship. My knees hit the boards below me, and I felt Octave's hand squeezing the back of my neck as the water clawed at my cheeks. I pounded my fists furiously on his leg behind me. The water was cold as sleet, and I tried not to think about the fact that this was the trough that the animals drank from. Finally, after several seconds, he grabbed my collar and yanked me out sharply. I spluttered for air, leaning my forehead against the wooden crate's rim. Once my breathing had returned to normal, I gritted my teeth, rounding on Octave.

"What the hell are you trying to do to me?" I cried, attempting to stand and quickly slipping on the water splashed on the wood beneath my feet, just catching myself on the rim of the trough, sharp splinters cutting into the palm of my hand. "You could have killed me!"

Octave looked unimpressed. "Don't be dramatic. Here's the real question: what the hell are you trying to do, boy? Talking like that to the captain. You got a good deal here; you shouldn't ruin that because you're up to something."

I froze. "I, uh—no sorry, not up to anything." I wilted slightly under his stare. "However, well...Métivier did look a bit guilty; I reckon he probably didn't scrub behind the masts again, so if you're looking for someone to drown he's probably the best choice—" I cut off as he grabbed my arm again and dragged me to the stairs, shuffling me down below hurriedly. The door to the sailor's cots was open, and I heard several of them jeer as I was dragged by.

We stopped in front of the hold, and Octave sneered down at me, sticking the key into the door, but not unlocking it yet.

"You should learn to stop talking," he snarled, his crooked tooth catching on his lip. "You should learn to respect those who deserve respect, or you'll go the rest of the voyage without your supper." He turned the key, pushing the door open. I turned to go in, but was stopped by his hand still on my arm. I looked at him as he leaned down, his mouth next to my ear, my vision blocked by his tangle of black hair. "And most importantly, boy, and don't you forget this: If you're going to steal food in front of the Captain, do try to be somewhat sneaky about it, you absolute dolt."

Speechless, I was shoved into the room, the door slamming shut, and the conversation ending with the final *click* of the door being locked.

Chapter Six

Orpheline and Sacha looked up as I was tossed into the room, Sacha's hands quickly slipping beneath his coat. They raised their eyebrows pointedly, as if to say, "Go to sleep, don't look at us, you know the routine."

I gritted my teeth together.

You've got one chance, I thought. *If you fail now, you'll never get so much as a cough out of them.*

"How are you both today?" I asked. They glowered, and I cringed as Orpheline spit into the corner of the room, sucking her lower lip into her mouth and chewing at it. I took a breath. "Yes, well...Ah! I see you've already eaten." I gestured to their empty wooden plate. "What do they bring you? Two slices of pork and a biscuit each? Some clean water?"

"How many times must we tell you," Orpheline began, her head tilted back and eyes closed. "We couldn't care less about anything you have to say—"

"Yes, yes, I know," I interrupted, before catching myself. This was the moment. "I just figure, you can't be full, can you? You could still eat, I'm sure." Orpheline opened her eyes, as Sacha's glare lessened to something more confused than angry.

"Oy, what are you on about?" he asked. I shrugged.

"I just thought you two might want something else to eat..." Reaching into my jacket, I pulled out the napkin from breakfast and sat down, crossing my legs and spreading the cloth out below me. Slowly, I opened the napkin, revealing the food within. Sacha's eyes widened a fraction, before they pulled tight into a squint, peering at me suspiciously.

"What are you playing at, L'Émule? You trying to get us in trouble?"

I rolled my eyes. "I'm trying to feed you. I thought..." I took a breath, straightening my back and looking at them straight on. "I thought we might play a game."

A moment passed. Sacha opened his mouth several times, before closing it tightly and squinting in confusion. Orpheline was looking at me as though I had suggested we all pull our toenails out together.

"What sort of a game...?" she asked slowly.

I grinned. "Well, I ask you questions. You answer them, and I give you some food. The more questions you answer, the more food you get."

"You want to pester us."

"I want to talk."

Sacha eyed the bread on my napkin warily. "That's ship bread; it's bound to be sour and full of holes."

"As will be the conversation I'm sure, so really it's a fair trade," I replied cheerily. I picked up one of the biscuits, taking a bite from it, and smirked as Sacha jolted forward an inch, his hand twitching at his side.

"Longer you delay, more I eat. We're all hungry here, mate," I told him, chewing on the stale bread. Sacha opened his mouth to speak.

"Don't." Sacha and I turned, eyeing Orpheline. She had turned her face to the side, glaring at the wall. Sacha seemed to deflate looking at her.

"Orpheline, c'mon, we can't just—"

"Are we really going to sell ourselves out for food? Is that where we are now? Bartering our pride to some two-bit idiot who can't even—"

"I'll play," Sacha interjected, leaning forward onto his knees and staring at me, more awake than I'd seen him so far this whole trip. I grinned.

"Good," I said, tearing off a piece of a biscuit. "First question then: Are you two homeless, or just poor?"

"Rude," Orpheline muttered, staring at the floor.

"We got a place, but we don't stay there much." Sacha pushed up the cuff on one sleeve, and continued talking. "We stay out mostly, but we don't have to."

"Why do you then?" I asked.

He shook his head. "That's another question, that is."

"Fine then, here you go." I tossed him the piece of bread and tore off a new one, holding it between my middle and pointer fingers. "Where do you go if not home?"

"Places."

"Not a good enough answer." I raised the bread to my lips.

"Taverns, inns, sometimes the dock. Mostly the dock."

I could tell he was uncomfortable answering the questions; his eyes were flicking between the floor, his sister, and the bread in my hands. I flicked the bread to him, watching as he ate it quickly.

"How'd you get caught?"

Sacha arched a dark eyebrow. "Excuse me?"

I shrugged. "You got caught, here on the ship. How'd they find you?"

"Octave," Sacha growled, slouching in a way that reminded me of a child pouting. "We hid in the ripped rigging toward the back of the ship. There are piles of it; we should have been fine. Octave found us less than an hour out to sea. We'd seen him around the docks before—he's cranky as they come."

I nodded, passing him his bread. He tried to give it to Orpheline, but she merely eyed it with disgust before turning her head away. The three of us sat, quiet for a few moments. I picked at the bread in front of me. Sacha went to take a bite of his piece before sighing, clamping his jaw shut and putting the biscuit in front of Orpheline, folding his arms.

"Why'd you do it?" I asked.

"Do what?" Sacha didn't look up. I stood, walking across the room to the bales of hay and sitting on top the highest stack.

"Why'd you stowaway on the *Tromperie*?"

The silence in the room was palpable. Sacha shifted his weight forward, leaning his head against his knee. I could tell that this was the one question he didn't want to answer and that only made me want to know all the more.

"I'd give you the pork for your answer," I told him. "The lot of it."

He eyed the meat for a moment, before sighing heavily and reaching his dirty palm out. "Meat first," he insisted. I tossed him the salt pork and sat back, watching as he took a large bite and chewed hungrily. Finally, he spoke.

"We made a mistake."

"Ha!" I jumped slightly at Orpheline's sudden bitter outburst. She remained facing the wall. Sacha's face glowed bright red.

"...*I* made a mistake," he muttered.

"How so?" I asked.

He looked back at Orpheline, who said nothing in his defense. He took another bite of the meat, before beginning again, slowly.

"There are rules—not rules really but...guidelines in what we do. In..."

"Thievery," I supplied for him.

He nodded, staring at his hands and looking distinctly uncomfortable with the whole situation. "Three, actually. And I messed up one or two."

"You messed up *all* of them," Orpheline snapped.

Sacha glared at her. "You want to tell 'im? I thought you were pursuing life as a mute."

"You can tell it, but don't leave out details because you don't want him to know how much of an idiot you are."

"What are the rules?" I asked eagerly, leaning forward on the edge of the hay bale. The two of them broke away from each other and stared at me, before Sacha deflated once more and rubbed a hand over his eyes, a lock of curly brown hair falling across his face. He raised a hand and began to recite.

"Don't pick the same person twice." He put up one finger. "Don't leave an impression." He ticked another finger off, his gaze on me sharpening. "And never, *never* steal something that somebody would be willing to die for."

The room was silent, and outside the door I heard some men pass by, laughing loudly. A breeze bled through the cracks in the wall and I shivered, pulling my jacket tighter around my shoulders, inhaling the scent of the ocean. I broke the silence first.

"Gee...how d'you mess up all of those at once?"

"Shut your mouth," Sacha snapped, glaring. Orpheline smirked and picked up the biscuit Sacha had placed in front of her, taking a bite. He huffed angrily and I grinned, his obvious frustration soothing slightly the annoyance I had been feeling over the past few days.

"There's a tavern," he began, folding his arms defensively across his chest. "It's in the center of Calais, behind the Town Hall. Phe and I go there sometimes in the evenings, 'cause there's always lots of men there, too drunk to watch their pockets." He jerked a thumb to Orpheline. "She does the first tug usually, and I do the second."

"The tug?" I asked.

He rolled his eyes. "If you got something in your pocket, and someone comes and grabs at it in one big snatch, you're going to feel it, aren't you? See, it usually takes two tugs to get something; the first tug to loosen the pocket or the purse, and the second tug to grab whatever's inside it. It's good then that there's the both of us, because it's a lot more obvious when the same person bumps into you twice."

"Dear God," I muttered, eyeing the two of them. "You've got a whole system, a whole scheme. You're right criminals, you are!"

"Oh, shut it," Orpheline snarled, still chewing the biscuit. She wiped a hand sharply across her lips. "It's not like we're stealing babies or somethin'."

I eyed her disdainfully, before nodding at Sacha to continue.

"It used to be a lot easier. Before, you could just slash the strings on a purse and run. But then everyone began sewing their purses into their garments, making these pockets. See, adults aren't so good at stealin' when they have to slip their big clumsy hands inside a pocket. Takes a special sort of talent to pick a pocket. Anyway, we're in *La Chaloupe*—that's the pub—and there's these men, about ten of them, and they're sitting around this big ol' table in the back of the pub, drinkin' and looking over some papers. Well, I see this one man, big oaf lookin' fella, and he's got his back to me, with this sack just hangin' off his hip, and he's not paying any mind to it. So I figure, coins; it's got to be full of them, it looks heavy as anything, and it's just hangin' there by some cord. I'm used to working with much more difficult tugs, so this should be nothing!

"So I look over and see Phe making the first tug on another guy toward the entrance, but he can't have anything more than a few pennies in his small pocket, so I ignore her and go back to the guy in front of me."

"Ignoring me was your first mistake," Orpheline says slowly. She's looking at him oddly, and I can't tell if she's bemused or angry.

"Oy, would you keep quiet?" Another chill breeze swept through the room, and the three of us shivered in unison. Sacha let out a noisy breath into his hands before rubbing them together. "So I go up to this group of men, and they're all shouting over each other. Well, I duck between my man and the man on his left, I pretend to be just some boy trying to look at the papers, and while I'm doing that, I pull out this," he said, reaching down to his boot. His face glowed with the first genuine excitement I had seen on him so far, as he rolled down the cuff of his boot and slipped from it a small knife. It was jagged, a little rusty, and in place of a handle it had a bit of cloth wrapped around one end, tied with a string. He held it up and looked at me expectantly, clearly waiting for me to pass some judgment. I cleared my throat.

"It's, eh, nice," I said, smiling stiffly at him. He grinned and looked to Orpheline, who stared blankly back at him.

"Made it myself," he said proudly, puffing his chest up a bit. "Found some old metal in a bin and sharpened it myself. It don't look like much but it does well in a tiff."

I bit my tongue, refraining from asking how many "tiffs" he had gotten himself out of with that scrap of metal. "So what did you do with it?"

"Right, well, I pull this out and start peering real obviously at their papers, and the man I'm tagging to pick pushes me back, of course, so I can't see the papers, and when he does that I "fall" into him, and all quick cut the cord on the sack and grab it, and before he knows what's happened, I'm runnin' out the door, Phe right behind me." He deflated slightly, slumping down once more. "It all would have been good and whatnot, really impressive, except, well…"

I nodded, "You got caught."

"I got recognized," he said, his face pinched in annoyance or embarrassment. "Three weeks ago, we're on the outskirts of the harbor, and who should walk by but this same man and his buddies, and they saw me."

I frowned, looking Sacha over. He was rather plain, and I was sure that in the darkness of a tavern he'd be even harder to commit to memory.

"How'd he recognize you, though? I thought you were supposed to be professionals."

Sacha remained quiet. I turned to Orpheline.

"What did he do?"

She smirked, before raising her hand up in front of her face. Dangling from it was the bandalore. Sacha flushed and reached into his pocket before groaning.

"We don't pick *each other,* Orpheline," he grumbled, snatching the toy from her hands.

"Sacha likes to make things, you may have noticed," Orpheline said exasperatedly, sounding much like my mother would when I came to the dinner table with my shoes still on. "He made this the day we were in La Chaloupe, and he hasn't put it down since. I suppose it's one of those motions that catches the eye."

"I didn't mean it," Sacha interjected. "I figured it wouldn't draw any attention."

"Obviously."

I cut in quickly. "So what happened when he spotted you?"

"What do you think, you dunce? He started chasing us. Ran fast for a clunky person, I'll give him that."

"Did he get you?"

Sacha sneered at me, and I flinched. "Obviously not. Would we be here if he had caught us? We were runnin' from him, and we lost him for a bit in the harbor, but we knew he'd catch up soon, being as fast as he was…Well, I saw some ship at the dock, and it was tied up and there was a hatch open toward the rear. It looked dark…empty, so I sort of just jumped in, pulled Phe in after me. Didn't know the ruddy thing would close, didn't know the ship was going to leave port."

Suddenly, a loud crash echoed outside the room, causing the three of us to jump. We sat, frozen, staring at the door, waiting for someone to come through it. No one did; outside more voices laughed and passed by, going on their way. We let out a collective sigh.

"Just some drunk sailor, falling over himself," said Orpheline, still eyeing the door wearily. "Idiots, the lot of them."

"They're not so bad," I replied quietly, rubbing my arm through my jacket in an attempt to heat it up. I winced as my palm touched a bruise that Octave had undoubtedly left there at some point.

Sacha let out a groan, rubbing a hand over his stomach. "I'm still starved. You couldn't have managed to get anything else into that ridiculous jacket of yours?"

I looked at my jacket. "It's not ridiculous, it's *tailored*. Besides, I took what I could get. I suppose I don't have your *expertise*," I sniped.

"Clearly not," Orpheline agreed. "We could have gotten a piece of roast."

I huffed, falling onto my back on the hay. Slivers of light streamed through cracks in the ceiling planks. I could see the shadows of feet moving above me, and I closed my eyes as dust sifted onto my face.

"How much money was it?" I asked after a moment.

"What?"

"In the sack that you took. How much money was it? Let's see it, then."

"Oh…" Sacha paused, and I sat up. He and Orpheline were looking at each other, having what I was sure was a very important silent conversation. Finally, Orpheline looked at me, and her mouth twisted slightly in hesitation.

"It wasn't, exactly, money," she said slowly.

I frowned, jumping down from the bale and moving over to where they sat. I sat down cross-legged in front of them. "All right then, if it wasn't money, what was it?"

Sacha seemed to grind his teeth momentarily before coming to some decision, lunging forward far enough to grab my collar. I groaned.

"Why does everybody on this ship seem so intent on injuring me?"

"Listen here." Sacha jabbed a bony finger under my chin. "I'm going to show you what it is, but only because if I don't, I know you're not going to shut up about it."

"You know me so well," I replied dryly.

He sized me up for a second longer before letting me go and nodding to Orpheline. Slowly he reached inside his coat and tugged, pulling from it a thick, leather bound book, no bigger than his palm. He handed it to me.

I looked at them skeptically, before focusing on the small book. It was simple, brown and well worn. The edges of the pages were stained in different colors, as if it had been flipped through at many a different meal. The leather had no writing on it, save for three letters carved into the spine, which read *"L.E.F"*. It was closed securely with a metal band around the body, fastened in the front with a small, iron lock.

Puzzled, I looked at the two of them, handing it back. "What's that supposed to be?"

Sacha shrugged, tucking the journal under his coat.

"No clue, but I'll tell you what—the way he chased us for it? It's probably a lot more important than some sack of coins."

Chapter Seven

"All right then, you two, budge up."

Orpheline and Sacha looked up as the door to the hold was locked behind me. We waited for a moment until the sound of Octave's footsteps faded away, before I moved to sit by them. Orpheline was perched with her back to the far left corner of the room, her knees drawn tightly to her; Sacha slumped with his back to the wall, his head tipped back; I faced them with my back to the door, my legs crossed in front of me. It was the same position we had been sitting in for the past two weeks, unchanging except for when one of us felt the need to stand and pace for several minutes to avoid going stir-crazy. I pulled a heavy white napkin from my coat and settled it between us.

"What took you so long?" Orpheline asked as I settled in front of them.

I huffed in lingering frustration. "The captain mentioned that he had a sore throat, and then Octave had the men and I searching high and low for a coughing syrup. We finally found one in the medic's cabin, which Métivier *said* he had checked. It took almost an hour and by the end of it the Captain found a private supply that apparently he had completely forgotten stowing in his cabin drawer."

"Figures, the bloody dolts." Sacha eyed the food eagerly. "You're getting better at this," he said, grabbing eagerly at a half-loaf of salted bread from the cloth as I unpacked our meal.

I grinned. "Worried I might put you out of a job?" I asked. He scoffed and began eating his bread. Orpheline looked intently at the selection of meat, chewing on her lip as if contemplating something very important.

"Mon Dieu, Orpheline," Sacha exclaimed, spitting a bit as he talked and chewed. "It's pork, not a game of wits. Just pick something and eat it."

Orpheline glared at him before grabbing a strip of salt pork and shoving it into her mouth, chewing with her mouth open.

"'Ou couldn' 'o it," she mumbled around the food. I glanced up from where I was tearing my piece of pork into bite-sized pieces.

"Excuse me?"

"Do our jobs. Be a pickpocket. You'd be rubbish at it." She said it all so matter-of-factly that I could do nothing but gape at her, trying to ignore how affronted I felt by the statement.

"I'm sure I could, but God only knows why I'd try," I retorted.

"Nah, she's right, she is," Sacha cut in. "You got a mark."

"I've got a what?"

"A mark." He tapped his right cheek with one finger, staring at me pointedly. "You've got a birthmark."

I realized, of course, what he was speaking about; a red blotch, the size of peach pit on my cheek. It was raised slightly and had been there for as long as I could remember.

"Ah. I suppose you're right..." I trailed off. Sacha smirked.

"Disappointed?"

"Hardly. I can only think of about ten hundred things I would rather be doing than sticking my hands in a stranger's pockets."

He laughed. "Well, don't turn it down till you've tried it, mate."

"I'm not your mate," I told him, nibbling on the edge of the meat. I was still full from dinner, but sitting in the hold doing nothing but talking was nearly unbearable. I was certain I'd gained at least a stone since I'd arrived on the ship. Mother would have to have my entire wardrobe re-sewn when I returned home. I wondered often why the other men on the ship complained about hunger, and I had a sinking suspicion that Dejafosse was giving me slightly more than the others, on the chance that I truly was what I told him. If that were the case, he would be pleased when we returned and my parents thanked him.

"What about your mates then?" I snapped out of my reverie and looked at Orpheline. She was peering at me behind dark hair.

I was at this point fairly confident in Sacha's ability to tolerate me. We had built a shaky, wavering, and temporary trust based completely on food, but at least he would speak to me freely. Orpheline, however, still regarded me as akin to a toad on her dinner plate and spoke to me as if I were a four year old with an undeveloped brain. I tried to return the favor. Why should I be good to her if she insisted on acting like a spoiled brat with me?

"What about them?"

"Have you got any?"

I glared at her. "Don't be *stupid,* Orpheline; I've got loads of friends. Absolute myriad friends, who are no doubt awaiting my return anxiously back…back at home."

I paused. I thought back to the boys I studied with. I had, at this time in my life, what I considered to be a gaggle of people with whom I conversed…whom I would refer to as my friends. The sheer concept of this girl, this…street rat having more friends—more acquaintances even—than I had was…preposterous. Sheer babble. I told her as much.

"What good are loads of friends," she spat, "if not a one of them would stand by you?"

"Stand by me?" I scoffed. "What are we, the French armada? We're children."

She stared at me for a long moment, and I felt my collar tighten under her gaze. Finally, she spoke.

"Would you, then, consider yourself a trustworthy ally?" she asked.

I rolled my eyes. "All right, if we're to be so serious, yes; I believe I am a more than worthy friend."

As I watched, she leaned forward, her palms sliding along the hard floor as she inched her way toward me. I glanced nervously at Sacha, who sat still, save for the *swoosh* of his bandalore, seemingly unmoved by his sister's looming presence near me.

"What would you do," she began slowly, "for those you care about?"

It was not, I supposed, a difficult question. I thought about my mother at home, and how worried she must be about me. I thought about my father, who I hadn't seen in more than a month, and how guilty he must feel for losing me.

He must have stayed at the harbor for days, searching for me, wondering where I had gone. Perhaps someone had seen me climb into the barrel. Perhaps they knew where I had gone…perhaps they were sitting at home in our living room with the draperies drawn and all callers turned away, already mourning a son they thought they had lost for good. I wished I could tell them. Call out over the waves that I was still here, doing well all things considered; scream that I would be with them in a heartbeat if I could just get off this damn ship! I swallowed the sudden lump in my throat and looked back to Orpheline.

"I can't think of anything I would not do for my family," I said.

She shook her head in annoyance, standing briskly and pacing across the room. I glanced at Sacha. Our eyes met, and I raised an eyebrow at him. He shrugged and turned back to Orpheline.

"Are you…quite all right?" I asked. She spun around to face me.

"Are you a complete idiot?" she hissed. I drew back in confusion. "No. Don't answer that. Why can't you just answer the question as I asked it?"

"I have! I said—"

"I didn't ask what you would do for your family; I asked what you would do for those you cared about? For those who were close to you."

"Aren't they the same thing?" I asked, growing agitated at her tone.

She shook her head, crossing her arms across the front panel of her nightgown. "They don't have to be."

I peered at her for a moment. I felt Sacha's gaze against the side of my face and thought back to those in my home who weren't my blood. I thought of what I did to get where I was; all the tutors who worked with me daily, the boys who played with me; my nanny who had cared for me until only a few years ago. I thought of what they had done for me. What I would do for them.

I looked Orpheline in the eyes.

"There is nothing I would not do for those that I care about."

We sat, the three of us, tense and silent for a long minute.

I stood, walking to the hay bales across the room, stretched out on the lowest one. "I'm going to sleep," I said, watching as Orpheline moved to the wall, sitting beside her brother. They said nothing, but as I closed my eyes, I thought I saw a smile gracing Orpheline's gaunt cheeks.

Chapter Eight

The next morning I realized that sometimes, you really think you know a person, and then they surprise you.

"Perhaps we got off on the wrong foot."

I looked at Orpheline incredulously from where I sat atop the wooden desk to the side of the room. She stood against the far wall, arms crossed and a thin smile crossing her thin face.

"Pardon?"

She shrugged, smile still firmly in place. "I just realize that you've been doing...a fair bit for the two of us, and I think it's time we all stop acting like four year olds and begin acting like three people stuck in the same lousy situation."

Part of me wanted to say no, to push the same unjustified anger that she had been shoving at me for the past two months back at her; to make her feel the frustrating sting of being ignored with as much strength as I had felt it. Alas, though I am many things, begrudging is not one of them.

"Yes," I agreed. "I reckon you're right. Not getting anywhere by arguing, are we?"

She smiled tightly. "No. No, we're not."

"Good, then, that's settled." I smiled back. A moment passed in silence. Then another. Sacha cleared his throat loudly.

"Well, I hate to be the one to ruin the ambiance but we're not really getting anywhere by *not* arguing either." He grabbed his leg as Orpheline kicked out at him, hitting his shin. "Oi!"

"Must you be so impatient?" she asked.

Sacha sneered at her. "I don't know, M'lady, *must* you be so kicky?" He spit into the corner of the room, and I grimaced. "Besides, I don't know what I'm supposed to be patient for. Shall I patiently await my execution? Patiently wait for them to tell me if it's a hanging or an axe?"

"Sacha!"

"What? Am I wrong?"

Orpheline huffed, turning away from him. "Must you be so glum?"

He snorted. "Oh, right. I'm ruining the cheery environment we've got here." He gestured at large to the dank room.

I chuckled, quickly trying to hide the sound behind my hand and a cough as Orpheline rounded on me.

"And what do you find so funny about this, eh?"

I stuttered, putting my hands out in defense. "No, I, uh—well…You're not actually to be hanged. They won't hang you just for being stowaways. They'll just…toss you off when we get to India. You'd have to do something truly awful to get hanged." Sacha was staring at me blankly. "Sorry to disappoint you, mate. You could always shoot someone! That would get you hanged for sure."

Orpheline rolled her eyes and walked toward me. She stuck a hand out, and I flinched, only for her to reach past me and grab my jacket.

"Excuse me, that's mine."

She moved to the desk, falling to her knees and crawling into the foot space. "I'm taking a nap. Keep your voices down," she muttered, balling up my jacket and resting it under her head.

I glanced over at Sacha to find that he had already pulled his bandalore from his pocket. "Let it go, Marin. Best to let sleeping dogs lie." He ducked as a boot flew at him, narrowly missing his left cheek. "See what I mean?"

✳✳✳

"Why haven't you opened it?"

The week had passed quickly. I had spent the majority of it with Octave on the upper decks. The winds had been picking up as of late, making the rigging susceptible to loosening and tears, and the men had taken to debating the probability of a sea storm hitting us as we rounded the horn of Africa. Deole believed the storms would hit us dead on, ending in a horrible shipwreck which would kill the majority of us and leave the rest gravely disfigured. Métivier, on the other hand, was slightly cheerier about the whole matter, proclaiming that he could feel bad storms in his knees, and that it would surely blow over long before it got to us.

Personally, I stood more in Deole's corner than Métivier's. The sky was grey as stone, and fog made it impossible to see more than a click ahead of us. I attempted to suggest switching course to something less…storm prone, but was quickly silenced by the rest of the crew's laughter, as well as Octave's advice that I should stick to topics I understood. He assured me, however, that if the men needed advice on how to make a nice cup of tea, they'd come to me first.

I found that the hours in the hold sped by now that I had the simple addition of conversation to the journey. Sacha had remained less than enthusiastic; a mere voice with whom I could pass the minutes talking. His contributions to the talks were minimal, usually sticking to one or two word answers.

"How much longer do you think we'll be on here?"

"A while."

"Do you miss home at all?"

"No."

"Do you ever grow tired of smelling like a barn?"

"Shut it."

Orpheline, on the other hand, was seemingly interested in nothing but my life. I found that she and I had a similar pattern of staying up late into the night, and where as Sacha spent the daytime pacing the hold restlessly, she and I much preferred sleeping during the day. My nights were soon filled with her questions about me.

"Do you have any siblings?"

"Yes. One."

"Is he as annoying as Sacha?"

"More so, if you can imagine."

"What will you do when you go home?"

"Eat a pie. A hot meat pie."

I found myself nervously appreciating her company. I was hesitant to put any real faith into a girl who had threatened to mutilate me during our first conversation, and yet since then she had taken such a dramatic turnaround in her opinion of me that it was quite hard not to be charmed by her. When interested, Orpheline could be fine to talk with, and although her brother resembled the type of person I spent time with back home, simple and immature as I could be occasionally, I couldn't deny that I was coming to enjoy my talks with Orpheline. Despite my tentative happiness, I could not deny my slight suspicion over the suddenness of her change of heart. With no reason to distrust her, though, I could do no more than amiably accept her friendship.

The questions came and went without much ado all week long. Then I asked the wrong question.

"What do you mean, why haven't we opened it?" Orpheline asked, looking up from where she was using a rusty nail to carve an ornate "O" in the floorboards.

I stood, walked to the desk and pulled open the single drawer below its surface. From it, I took out the stolen journal, holding it up for them to see. Sacha—lying on his back, trying to catch dust as it fell from the rafters—tensed as he spotted the journal. Orpheline remained blank faced.

"Oh, that."

Sacha sat quickly, brushing off his coat. "Why would we need to open it?"

I looked at him skeptically. "Why wouldn't you *want* to open it? You're two of the nosiest people I've ever met! I can't believe that you haven't even tried to see what's inside."

"We're already in enough trouble as it is," Orpheline said dismissively, returning to her carving. "Besides…"

I waited expectantly. "…Besides?"

"Besides," she continued. "…We don't know how to."

I barked a laugh, unable to help myself. Surely she was joking? A glance at her stony face was enough to show that she was, in fact, not.

"You're kidding," I said, still grinning despite myself. "No! Surely two thieves of your *amazing* prowess know how to pick a simple lock like this one?" I waved the journal around once more. Sacha, apparently done being insulted, stood and walked over to me, snatching the journal from my hand and tucking it back into the folds of his coat. Orpheline, cheeks now tinted pink, muttered into her hands.

"We pick pockets, not locks."

I felt oddly elated by their lack of ability to open the journal. "Why don't you break it open?"

Sacha snorted, his arms crossed defensively. "No problem, sure, we'll just try that. It's not like the band is solid iron or anything. I'm sure we can manage if we all try *really hard.*"

"But how do you know if you don't—"

"L'Émule!"

The three of us jumped violently as Octave's voice thundered through the room. The pounding of his fists echoed off the walls and rang in our ears.

"Get out of there *now,* boy, and I might let you live yet."

"Is it just me," I began quietly, "or does he sound angrier than usual?"

"I wonder what you did to annoy him," Sacha mused, looking less than interested in my worries.

"Yes," Orpheline added, "it's not as though you've been stealing food from him or anything."

"L'Émule, NOW."

I blanched and jumped to my feet, scurrying toward the door and rapping twice to signify I was there. It swung open, and I was grabbed without another word. Octave dragged me into the hallway then locked the door. He tugged me along so fast that I struggled not to fall over my own feet. I tried to hear him as he muttered beneath his breath. "Of all the stupid...couldn't wait three damn hours...not my fault if he..."

We reached the top deck and began briskly moving across it. I stared with blooming fear at the majority of the ship's men, lined up and at attention. With a sense of foreboding I took in their solemn faces. Stealing a glance at the end of the line, I felt a final blow to my gut—Dejafosse stood in front of the steps to his cabin, a scowl on his face and a whip in his hand.

Chapter Nine

The wind slapped against my cheeks, and my nostrils began to burn as I inhaled the salty ocean spray. Dejafosse stared straight ahead, his demeanor stony and eyes unapologetic.

Octave and I stopped about two feet in front of the captain. Octave's face was void of emotion, his body relaxed and yet the stingingly tight grip on my arm gave him away. I shook slightly as Dejafosse began to speak.

"I run my ship fairly," he began. "I run my ship with rules and with order. There is a way that we behave here…and there are many ways we do not. If a man who works on my ship defies my orders, there are consequences." He slid his palm down the length of the tan whip, his gaze firm and unwavering. I trembled in Octave's grip. "If a man who works on my ship attempts to lie to me, there are consequences." He released the tail end of the lash, and I swallowed thickly as it hit the floor. "And if a man who works on my ship steals from me, there are *severe* consequences."

I felt Octave suck in a breath at my side, and his grip tightened further. Dejafosse gestured to the men lined up on the ship, and I turned to look at them. Deole stood near the front, his face tight, as if he was working to remain as unperturbed as Dejafosse was. Métivier stood farther toward the stern of the ship, with some of the younger men, his hands clenched at his side and his face turned slightly away from me.

"Look at these men, boy. These hardworking men. When you were stealin' all that food, did you ever wonder who you were stealin' it from?"

I felt a creeping shame forming in my chest. I hadn't thought of it. I hadn't thought of it at all. I had been so caught up in the game of making people like me that I had completely forgotten that food didn't come to these men like it did to me at my home. Dejafosse continued to speak.

"Do you know how many meals you've taken from the mouths of these men?"

When the food ran out on this ship, they couldn't get any more of it.

"Do you think you've earned more than they have? By sitting around on your arse all day doing nothing?"

I'd been taking food for myself, Sacha and Orpheline, in addition to the meals I was given, and these men might end up getting nothing. I looked to Métivier and the other young men, who were more skin than fat, and wondered if I had in any way done that to them...

"Whatever your thinking was, which I'm sure was minimal, you have done a misdeed to your fellow men, and to me, after I so kindly allowed you safe passage aboard my vessel. I would not grant pardon to my men, so I must not grant pardon to you, either. It will be four lashings. Remove your shirt."

He stepped back, signaling two of his sailors to bring a wooden bar, slightly higher than my neck. I knew what would happen next. I had been witness to only one whipping in my life, at a dinner party my mother had taken me to. I was only eleven then, but the worker who had so foolishly—innocently—dropped the dishes screamed so loudly that I could still hear his shrieks in my ears.

I raised my pale hands to my chest to remove my shirt, but found my fingers were shaking too violently to grasp the buttons. I bit my lip to stop the trembling, and the eyes of the men behind me burned into my back. I finished the third button around the neck, and went to pull the shirt over my head when I felt Octave's hand release my arm. A rush of warmth flooded my fingers as the blood began to pump into them once more, and the hand that had been on my arm a moment before came to rest on my shoulder.

"Captain, if I may."

Both Dejafosse and I turned to look at Octave as he spoke, voice firm but quiet. Dejafosse raised an eyebrow at him.

"The boy's a rat, there's no denying that," he began, glancing at me down his nose. "And an idiot on top of it. The worst part of him, however, is that he just don't know how much of an idiot he is." Dejafosse eyed Octave warily as he spoke. "You would punish any of your men had they done something so foolish as this, but this boy is not one of your men. A stupid child, and one who meant no harm."

The captain shook his head. "We cannot let him go without—"

"He will not go without, Captain, I assure you. I merely ask that you grant slight pardon to the boy. Let him stay below deck a week and take away his supper. Give him enough breakfast to get him through the day and no more, but Captain—does whipping a boy like this do anything but make him more stubborn?"

"It's always worked in the past," Dejafosse grunted, his fingers still twitching the whip's handle. Octave shook his head.

"Not always."

The deck went silent. I watched avidly as the two men looked at each other, unblinking, and I had the feeling that more was being said than I understood. Though my trembling had faded away, I stayed tense, waiting to see who would break first. Behind me I thought I heard a low whistle from one of the men. Finally, after several moments, Dejafosse sighed, scrubbing a hand over his eyes.

"You are needed on the deck each day, Octave, so who shall watch the boy?"

"I'll do it, Captain."

There was a rustle as the men turned, myself included, to look at Deole who stood with a hand raised slightly. He smiled down at me, and I felt all the tension run out of my chest. It was the type of smile you see on a man who has known far worse than the troubles at hand.

Dejafosse seemed pensive for a moment, and I feared he was changing his mind about the lashings. Finally, he waved dismissively at Deole, turning on his heel and beginning the march up to his rooms. "Fine, then. For the next week you'll wake up before dawn, eat your bread—which will be brought to you—then report to Deole below decks to assist with the manning of the capstan. You will remain there for the duration of the day and return to your cabin in the evening, before the men have their dinners. Do I make myself perfectly clear?"

He turned to me slightly as he pulled the door to his cabin open, and I swallowed, nodding.

"Perfectly, Captain."

✻✻✻

With Deole as my guide, I made an astute observation the next day: I knew absolutely nothing about ships. Before I boarded the *Tromperie*, I had thought ships were wood, staying afloat and moving through the interaction of wind and sails. A few ropes, a few men, but nothing to sing about, surely. Within the first two months of my time on the ship I had discovered a plethora of features I had no idea ships held: canons, and halls that wound and dipped, and men from every branch of life—lifelong sailors and newcomers like Métivier. Tools and tricks—but none of that had interested me or caught my attention as much as the capstan.

Below the center of the top deck was a room, dank and plagued with must and humidity. It was sparsely filled, nothing but a closet door to its back, a wall of hooks from which devices I had never seen hung and dangled, and falling from its ceiling, a mammoth, rusting, iron mantle, from which four large wooden beams protruded out in every direction like a wheel.

My first day inside the room was spent being shown the workings of the job.

"Yuh see, the ropes need to go around your arms. The strain would rip your hands apart."

"See, these help keep the ship on course."

"Clockwise turns. Counterclockwise an' the ship takes a nasty tumble."

By midday my stomach was clawing at my insides, and my arms were so sore I feared they might fall off. The ropes we tied to the beams were thick and fastened over our clothes as not to give us burns, however the strain itself was pain enough.

Through the cracks in the ceiling, I watched the light of day begin to fade, and it was with exhausted relief that I bid Deole goodnight and followed Octave back to the hold.

He and I walked in a tense silence, and the sound of our boots hitting the floorboards beneath us echoed off the thin walls. I felt the disappointment sizzling off him in waves, and I began to curl in on myself. I preferred it when adults got angry. My parents in particular; angry adults are possible to handle. Adults when disappointed are miserable.

As we neared the door, I couldn't contain myself any longer. I turned to Octave.

"I'm sorry. I didn't mean for that—"

"Don't," he hissed, his teeth clenched together. "Don't apologize to me. I warned you, you stupid boy. I warned you to be careful, to not—don't apologize, just get in your damn room." He walked quickly to the door and unlocked it.

I walked in, Orpheline and Sacha looking up at me from the wall. The door closed behind me and I spun around, pressing my hands to the wooden surface. I heard Octave rattling the keys on the other side.

"Octave, can you hear me?" No response. "Octave…Thank you." There was nothing but a heavy silence for a minute, before I heard the click of the lock being turned, and Octave's steps echoing down the hall and away from the hold.

Chapter Ten

"How do your fingers not fall off? I swear this is torture."

Deole smiled, his jaw muscles working as we continued to move, the ropes around our arms constricting tightly as we continued our pacing. The capstan was grinding loudly in my right ear, and my jacket and shirt had long since been discarded in an attempt to save them from the buckets of sweat streaming down my body. Deole seemed much better off than I, for he had taken only one break since we began that morning, and he had yet to break more than a light sweat.

We made another rotation around the room, and as I passed by the door for what may have been the hundredth time that day, I heard the laughter of men as they walked by, heading toward the galley for dinner. I stopped absently, gazing longingly at the door that led to open air. My stomach rolled, and I grimaced in hunger.

"Maybe we should stop for today," Deole said from the other side of the capstan. I smiled apologetically.

"No, I'm sorry, we really should keep going…"

He chuckled, reaching up to untie the rope from around his arm, gesturing with his hand for me to do the same. Once we were both free, he began to dissemble the wooden beams.

"Help with this, boy. I am older now, it is not so easy anymore."

I moved over to help him with the first beam, the sore muscles in my arm quivering under the weight of it. I let out a shaky laugh. "I can't believe you do this by yourself usually."

"I don't," he said, as we lowered the plank to the floor, pushing it to the far end of the room. "Usually I have one of the boys to help me, but you offered so politely I had to take you on." He winked at me and I flushed, still rather put out about the public rebuke I had received.

"Do you think the men are still laughing at me?"

He laughed out loud at that, his dark skin glinting slightly under the streams of light through the cracks above. "Boy, we are sailors. We laugh at e'erybody. Don' worry though, they goin'ta get tired of you real soon, start makin' fun of someone else."

"They don't laugh at you," I told him, moving to slide the next beam out of its place.

"Boy, I am older than this ship itself. Who is goin'ta laugh at me?" He shook his head, rough hands grabbing the beam firmly, steadily moving it to the floor to join the first. "I been here for many years, done a lot a' jobs. I been a swabbie, I been a first mate, I been an ironsmith, and a cook! I seen enough men come an' go to know that I like it down here. I been here long enough to know you pick your battles wisely." He pointed at me with a bony finger. "Where as *you,* do *not* pick your battles wisely."

I huffed, brushing the wooden flakes off my hands, before shoving them into my pockets to cool down. I had never quite met a man like Deole before, all calm words and tone of voice, and a complete lack of worry about anything. I appreciated that attitude. That and the sheer amount of things he had done! The cooking and cleaning and—

"I'm sorry, but did you say you were an ironsmith?"

He looked up from where he was tying off the rope onto the middle shaft of the capstan. "Aye, for a good ten years of my life. From Rotterdam to Java and back again."

My heart began to race. I tried to sound as nonchalant as possible. "So then, you know all sorts of tricks, right? Like…mending hinges, or fixing barrels…or opening locks?"

"All that and more. I wouldn't still be on board if I were not good at what I did. Damn." He paused, eyeing the rope in his hands. "This rope isn't goin'ta be strong enough to last long."

I nodded, turning back to my length of rope, still hanging beside me from the mantle. I should probably have tied it off already and yet…

"I don't suppose you could…show me any of that, could you?"

He froze, looking at me with an odd glint in his eye. "Why? Yuh want to learn to fix a barrel? The one you came in on a bit rusty then?"

"Uh…no. That is to say…if you'd like to teach me that, I'd be more than interested, but I actually meant more of the, um…well, the lock opening bit."

He nodded slowly. "Uh-huh, I see…and why would yuh want to know a thing like that?" he asked, his hands working the rope steadily.

I shrugged, my clammy hands clenching nervously in my pockets. "Seems like a useful thing to know."

Deole grinned, wrapping the rope tight around his wrinkled right hand. He pulled it taught, and I heard the creak of the wood overhead as the rafters were worked.

"Marin, boy, you a terrible liar," he croaked. "You are goin'ta need a better excuse than that." He passed me the second rope, which had been dangling uselessly at my side, and I took it, sliding forward a bit as the force of it yanked me hard. I thought for a passable excuse as we set the rigging. My palms began to burn as the rough ropes clawed at them viciously.

"It's boring down there. Three prisoners, nothing in common, nothing to do. Something like this could give me something to…show off. Couldn't I just have this one thing? It might keep me quiet. Keep me out of the way. You won't have to deal with me anymore."

Deole smiled indulgently, his deep brown skin stretching out over sharp cheekbones. "I don' mind yuh too much, boy; you get your work done on time. Extra pair of hands never hurt."

I groaned quietly, turning back to the ropes. Deole watched me work steadily for a moment, before reaching out and grabbing the cords from my hand. I looked on, confused as he moved to the side, around the wheel and to the peg-laden wall across the room. He tied off the ropes with confident hands, before nodding me over to follow him. I went slowly, still feeling slightly dejected at my mission's failure. Deole and I stopped in front of an old wooden door, which came up to just below my chin, and closed with a large brass lock. I waited as Deole pulled a small brass key from around his neck, oiled fingers slipping slightly as he used it to open the door, revealing a small closet; four feet deep and bare save for a small pile of ropes in the far corner. I felt Deole's hand clasp my shoulder.

"Would you mind fetching that rope for me, boy?" he asked, stretching his arms behind his back until the joints cracked. "My ol' knees are no good for crawlin' along these boards anymore."

I nodded, crouching low and slipping into the small space. I squinted in the dim light and reached out to grasp at the rope.

I spun around as I heard the door slam behind me, losing my balance and falling back, throwing my hands out behind me to catch my fall.

"D-Deole?" I paused, looking at the slit of light coming from under the door.

"I'm goin'ta slip something beneath the door; make sure you grab it."

I sighed in relief upon hearing his voice. "Deole? Not to be rude or anything, but could you let me out now?"

"No."

I stared at the door incredulously. "No?"

"You wanted to learn to pick locks, boy? Well, this is how you goin'ta do it."

Despite my initial panic at being trapped in such a confined space, I still shivered with a rush of excitement at the idea of what I was about to learn. The closet was hot and smelled of fish, yet chills swept over my bare shoulders. A rustle and light scrape sounded by my feet, and I leaned forward, fingers scrambling at the crack under the door. Then,

I felt them: two small pins, each the length of my middle finger.

Deole spoke. "You find those pins, boy?"

I sighed in relief and nodded, before remembering he couldn't see me. "I found them."

"Good, now put one in your right hand and one in your left."

I squinted at my hands in the dark and separated the two pins. As my eyes slowly adjusted, I realized what the pins were from. They were the type generally use to hold rope to the walls. With one in each hand, I knelt so that my right eye was aligned with the keyhole. "What do I do now?" I asked through the door.

"It's a lot easier than you think," he called. "Take one pin and push it into the keyhole as far as you can manage to squeeze it, then press down."

I followed the order, inserting the first pin into the square bottom of the keyhole. I felt the cool metal slide along my finger tips and shivered. I pressed down and heard a faint click. "Done. Is...is that it?"

I heard a chuckle from outside the door. "Not yet, boy, don't rush it. Now, that second pin; I need yuh to bend the end of it, just a bit." I gripped the end of the second pin between my left thumb and forefinger and pulled. Just as I felt the end begin to give way, there was a sudden, searing pain in my thumb.

"Damn it," I hissed, jerking my now punctured finger away and sucking it into my mouth.

"You all right there, boy?"

I made a sound of agreement, still suckling the cut slightly. I realized that, were I home, I'd have been fetched a bandage for it so quickly that it wouldn't have had time to start bleeding. I wondered what Mother would do if she could see me at that moment, crouched in the rotting rigging closet of a ship, sucking the wound from my thumb as I attempted to pick a lock open.

She'd probably keel over.

"Now, take that second pin and put it above the other. There's a latch at the top, and you goin'ta find it. It might take a minute or two. When you feel it, you goin'ta need to press up on it. Tell me when you find it."

Gingerly minding my thumb, I pushed the second pin—bend first—into the hole above the first and began to search for the latch. It was silent for a moment, the sole noise being the clicks of the lock.

"Why are you doing this?" I asked quietly. Deole let out what sounded like a cross between a laugh and a sigh.

"You're no stowaway, boy. I seen enough sneaks on these ships to know that you're nothin' more than a boy who wants back on land quick as possible." He paused, and I wiped my sweaty brow. "You know who you remind me of, boy?" Another pause as I continued to fumble with the lock. I heard a loud scraping, followed by a thump, and I imagined Deole had pulled a crate over to sit upon.

"Who?" I asked, as I continued to jab at the lock.

"When I first started on ships, I was about your age. I lived in Kingston, in Jamaica, before I came aboard, and I helped my father down in the shipyard. He was a fisherman, you see, and I was needed to lift and carry to heavy crates down to the docks to load on ships. I think back on my childhood and all I remember is the smell of fish rotting." He took a deep breath, giving me the sense that he wants his story to last as long as it takes me to get the lock open.

"So I am about fourteen years of age when I wake up in the middle of the night, to women screamin'. They saying that a ship crashed offshore against the rocks. A French ship. A royal ship. My father has me running outside in my skivvies, to get in a boat with the other men and pull survivors back to shore. Well, we get a few of them in our house till they get another ship, and one man—Amadour was his name—well, he and I became good friends, and he offered me a job on the ship, pulling fish. I, who had never left shore nor never thought I might, just about jumped outta my dried skin at the offer. A fortnight later, and I was aboard the king's ship Côme, with enough blisters to make a grown man cry and the surety that I did not want to be there anymore.

"I thought about getting off. After four months, we stopped in some northern French port and decided to spend a few nights there and warm ourselves by the local fires. After drinking their wine and talking to the native girls, I had all but decided to end my time as a sailor. That it was not the life for me. But then the damnedest thing happened—we found a stowaway.

"Hidden in the cook's salt barrel, there was this small, lanky little creature, his eyes wild and desperate, and his way was rabid. Clothes too good to be an orphan, manners too poor to be civilized, he threw us all into a frenzy. We took him to the captain—Dejafosse's father, true enough—who shouted at him with a rage I hadn't ever seen on the old man.

Kicking and spitting, he was, as we put him off the ship. We set out that night, and in all the excitement, I forgot to pack my bags and leave."

I heard a click from the lock and grinned, only to find no give as I jiggled the doorknob. Resting my head against the door for a moment, I tried to ignore the sweat spilling slowly down my back in this hot, small closet. Deole continued to speak, his voice airy and dreamlike, and I wondered if possibly he had forgotten all about me and returned to this time long before I existed. I lifted my head and turned back to my pins.

"Well, we pitched out that night for Spain, and I admit I was excited, and it's about three days into our trip when ol' Éloy starts shrieking that there's a boy in the goat pen. I thought he was lying—Éloy was as crazy as they come—but sure enough there's that same boy from the port, caught by his collar and cursing the crew. The captain locks him in a hold, feeds him, gives him water, and when we reach Spain, we toss the boy off the ship again, half a mile to shore, and make him swim back to land.

"We head off to Calais to restock for a trip we were goin'ta make down to Africa, and would you believe that a week later a younger mate gets sick while cleaning the captain's cabin, and when the cook goes to grab the spare bedding he finds that same damned boy, sleeping soundly on the extra sheets!" At this, Deole began to guffaw loudly, and I heard the slap of a hand on the knee as he continued. I waited for him to calm himself, gritting my teeth and working steadfastly at the lock. "So this time the captain don't yell; he just turns right around and walks away, back to his cabin and closes the door.

"We all real scared now, waiting for him to come out with a rifle and shoot the poor boy. But he doesn't. He doesn't come out for two days, and when he does, he walks straight to where this boy is scrubbing the decks and asks, 'Why?' and the boy turns red, and mutters, 'I like ships.' The Captain just looks real hard at him and says, 'I could throw you off when we get to Calais' and the boy says 'You know I'll just get back on. You know I will.' And I supposed the captain did know, because he nodded and rubbed his wrinkly chin and goes, 'I could throw you off here and now.' We all watched close, as this boy got up, and looked the captain dead in the eyes, and says to him, "Lock me up if you want, but you keep me on this ship. Put me in the lowest holds, hang me on the highest mast, but you keep me on this ship. I don't plan on touchin' dry land again until I'm bein' buried in it.'"

I hear the lock let off a quiet *tick* and I freeze, slowly turning the door handle and feeling it give way beneath my fingers. I let out a breath of excitement, but stay crouched, finding it impossible to pull away from Deole's story now.

"So you remind me of him. Not that you've shown any great enthusiasm to be here, but because you both stubborn boys. And that stubbornness is never goin'ta get you anything but trouble."

Chapter Eleven

"Let me open it."

"Not a chance."

I groaned loudly, falling backwards until I was lying flat on the bales of hay. In the few short hours since I had emerged from the closet and bid Deole goodnight, I had exhausted myself attempting to sway Sacha and Orpheline into giving me the journal to open. My efforts had been fruitless.

"You don't understand," I pleaded. "I sat in a closet for ten minutes to learn how to do this. You've got to let me."

Orpheline coughed harshly into her hand, before lowering her arm and looking down her nose at me. She said, "You sat in a closet for ten minutes because you were caught foolishly stealing food from the captain."

I stared at her in disbelief. "I was stealing it for *you* lot!"

"Oy!" Sacha said, wagging a finger in my direction and giving me a stern look that seemed entirely unsuited to his young face. "Don't you blame us for your immoral actions." Pulling it from my foot, I tossed my shoe at him, narrowly missing his head by a few inches. He continued, ignoring his near decapitation. "Your condemned soul aside, we're still not letting you open the journal."

"Why not? You've yet to give me one good reason."

"We've given you plenty!" Orpheline interjected, as she let out another bout of coughs. "You've just chosen to ignore them."

I huffed and rolled to my side to face the wall. Despite my nearly unbearable longing to discover the contents of that journal, I would have to be a fool not to realize the obvious risks for these two should the journal be opened. They were the ones who had been seen stealing the thing. Should it come to light, the men who had been robbed would surely come after these two. They'd either die at the hands of the men they robbed or the king's men who now held them captive. Neither was a good choice.

Probable death beside the point, there was no guarantee the journal would hold anything of any value. It could just be some man's petty diary. Sure, he had chased the siblings half way across the city for it, but perhaps because he had written about some nagging worry of his, of no concern to anybody else, that would be detrimental for him were it taken. Perhaps he'd cheated in a game of dice and then written it down for posterity. I couldn't even lay a finger on why I wanted so desperately to see the contents; I just knew that with every passing day locked away my longing grew stronger. My resolve had been slowly crumbling, and now that I had the ability to open the journal, the idea that they wouldn't let me was torture.

"It's not even *your* journal; why should you have any say in who opens it?"

Sacha raised an eyebrow, looking entirely un-swayed. He said, "It is ours. We stole it fair and square. Actually, I stole it, so really it's mine, but out of generosity I choose to share it with my dear sister."

"Smart thinking," Orpheline commented.

"Right. So those are the rules."

"Your rules," I said. "The king's rules say that this book now belongs to the royal guards until they find the original owner."

Sacha chuckled, tilting his head down to his chest and closing his eyes. "Yes, well, you may have noticed that Phe and I don't really make a habit of abiding by the king's rules."

"Yes, and look where that's gotten you," I muttered. The room went silent for a few moments, before Orpheline burst into another fit of coughs that wracked her body so violently she curled in on herself. I sat up and peered at her. "What on earth is wrong with you?"

She glared at me, but her watery eyes and rather pink nose made her more pathetic than threatening. "What does it look like, you ponce? I'm sick."

"You were perfectly fine yesterday."

"Everybody is perfectly fine until they get ill," she griped. I looked at her pointedly, and she deflated slightly. "It's my throat."

"That would explain the coughing."

Sacha scooted across the floor, throwing an arm over Orpheline's shoulders. "If you've got nothing of import to say, try not to say anything." He closed his eyes once more as Orpheline tucked her face into his shoulder. The two of them did not speak again.

I sighed heavily, resigning myself to another quiet night. The wind blew through the wall, and I silently wished, as I had many times in the past few months, to be home in my warm bed beneath my blankets. I wiggled my cold toes.

"Could one of you at least toss me my shoe back?"

***

I woke up planning. From the moonlight streaming through the wall and onto my clothes, I could tell that it was still the middle of the night. Across the room, Orpheline and Sacha still slumbered on, looking like two stray pups huddling for warmth. Before I knew what I was doing I was on my feet, slipping silently across the floor to the door. Lifting my hands to the top of my head, I ran my fingers over my scalp until I felt the two pins Deole had given to me and conveniently "forgotten" to retrieve. Kneeling so that I was level with the lock, I went to work as quietly as I could, and in only a matter of minutes I felt the mechanisms give. I stood. I pulled the door open as silently as possible, stopping with each squeak to check that the other two were still sleeping. Seeing no sign of movement, I left the room, closing the door gently behind me. While it made an audible *clunk* as it closed, I didn't want to risk a sailor walking by and seeing the door open.

Moving quietly I made sure to keep my back to the wall. As I felt the chill of the dank wood along my spine, it occurred to me how recently ago I had nearly lost some of my tender flesh to a whipping for my misbehavior, and now here I was, sneaking out of my room late at night—with every intention of even worse deeds this time.

The deck was empty as I reached the top of the steps, save for a grey-bearded sailor named Gérard who was manning the crow's nest high above, and Métivier, who sat slumped over with his back against the ship's side rail, asleep at his watch post. Pulling my coat tight around me I stepped as softly as I could, I glimpsed the Captain's quarters mere distance away. I held my breath as I reached the foot of the crow's nest and looked upwards, trying to identify which direction Gérard was gazing. If he was looking toward the stern, where I had come from, it was most likely safe to move forward. However, I reasoned, *were* he looking toward the stern he probably would have seen me approaching. Chances were he was looking ahead of the ship, eyes on the course in front of us. Were that the case, I'd have a hard time getting past him.

Then it struck me, the most absurd notion I had gotten since arriving on this ship—what would Sacha and Orpheline do? I glanced back at the entrance to the stairs below, as if the two of them were standing there, egging me on and miming the obvious solution to my dilemma. They weren't, of course; they were downstairs fast asleep, probably dreaming of a time when they weren't trapped aboard a smelly ship with some random stranger.

Turning back to the problem at hand, I closed my eyes and shook my head to clear my thoughts. I considered making a run for it, but with no distraction I'd be caught for sure. Past the stairs to the hold, I could hear the laughter of the men still awake, drifting up from the entrance to the galley. I began to tap my foot softly in frustration, running a hand through my hair. My eyes snapped open.

Breathing through my nose as softly as possible, I lifted my right foot, leaning my back to the mast for balance, and began to unlace my boot, pulling it from my foot and tucking it beneath my arm. Repeating the motion with my left foot, I took the first boot in hand and, praying silently, threw it across the deck toward the stairs to the galley, watching as it crashed into several crates, knocking them off kilter.

"Oy? Who's down there?" I didn't breathe as Gérard called out from above me. I simply stood, unmoving against the mast. I waited several seconds, gripping my second boot to my chest. Finally, I heard it—a bark of laughter from one of the men below. Alongside the howling wind that danced across the ship, it was almost impossible to tell that the laughter was coming from below decks. The wild air seemed to carry the noise in every direction. As it echoed across the deck, I prayed to God and my mother that this worked, then chucked the second boot to the same place as before. It struck another crate, one that held the dried meats, and I flinched as the crate crashed down the stairs. If I was correct, it would be just loud enough for Gérard to hear, but not so loud as to attract the other men. Several seconds passed. Finally, I heard a *whoop* sound from above, and Gérard's amused voice thundered over the deck.

"Ah, go back down to your bread and your ale, you drunk bastards! You'll break your necks up here in all this wet!" I didn't wait to make sure he was looking to the galley door. I simply chose to believe that he would face the direction of his taunts. Without looking back, I dashed from the mast, toward the captain's quarters. Taking the three steps to his doorway in one leap, I landed as soft as I could on my toes. As I pulled the pins from my hair once more, I hoped beyond hope that the captain was down with Octave and the rest of his crew in the galley, rather than asleep in his bed.

With the haunting memory of Dejafosse's face as he held a whip in his hand, I slipped quietly through the now unlocked door and into the captain's quarters.

Chapter Twelve

Sacha and Orpheline stared at me in confusion. To be fair, I had woken them only a moment before, and I was now holding some unknown bottle at them. Orpheline began to cough, but still did not take her eyes from the bottle. Once her coughs had subsided, I waved it at her once more.

"Well?" I asked, grinning broadly. "Don't you want to know what it is?"

"Yes." "No." Sacha and Orpheline spoke at the same time. I shrugged and turned to Sacha.

"All right, then, I'll just tell you. It's syrup. A syrup for what, you ask? A syrup for coughing if you must know." Without waiting for him to pause, I went on quickly, tossing the bottle a little and catching it again in my palm, smirking as I saw Orpheline's eyes follow the motion. "I took it. I'm sure you'd like to know how I took it—"

"Most likely very poorly," Orpheline interjected.

"—but that is something I must keep to myself. However! I can tell you why I took it."

"For that nasty cough of yours?" Sacha asked dryly.

"No. For that nasty cough of your sister's." Without taking my eyes off of Sacha, I threw the bottle to Orpheline, who caught it in her cupped hands.

Her eyes grew wide for a moment before narrowing. She asked, "What do you want?"

"What do you mean?"

"For this. You must want something. More answers, more information, my first-born son—something."

I shook my head, going over to lean against the back wall of the room. "Nothing. Just…nothing. Don't mention it."

"No," Sacha interjected. "Could this really be an act of *friendship*? From you?"

I scoffed. "God, no. Just think of it as you…owing me a favor one of these days." I glanced at Orpheline and watched as she swallowed the coughing syrup in two gulps. I whistled. "You know, I think you're supposed to have a sip of that. If you take it all like that, you'll pass out."

She stuck out her tongue at me and glared, and it looked so much like the faces I would make at my older brother when we were children, that I couldn't help but stick my tongue out at her in return. She tossed the bottle back to me, and I stuck it in my left pants pocket, before closing my eyes and folding my hands behind my head. We sat quietly and listened to the raging wind outside. Orpheline was swallowing periodically, most likely to test her throat for soreness. My eyes having been closed for several minutes, I jumped slightly when Sacha piped up from his corner.

"Where are we going? Do you know?" I stared blankly at him. "The ship, I mean. The sailors talk to you, so they must have told you."

"Oh, right. India," I said, then paused. "We're rounding the eastern edge of Africa now, though. We'll be stopping here first. Then India."

"Why are we stopping here?" he asked quickly, and I noticed Orpheline lean forward. It struck me that this might be the first information they had received since coming aboard the ship.

"We're taking on another passenger." I thought back to what Octave had told me several weeks before. "A general. He's the one who will be helping us make the trade. Deole says that he's dealt with the merchants in Pondicherry many times. What's more, he has weapons. He's giving them to the King, since he apparently has no use for them now that he's left his position. So we'll be picking him up in three day's time, and he'll be coming with us to Pondicherry, and then we're to bring him back to France."

"And how will he return to Paris?"

I looked up in surprise as Orpheline spoke. "Your throat better then?"

"It is, yes. So how is he getting to Paris?"

"I don't know," I told her, bristling at her dismissive tone. "I think he's managing that for himself, but I don't know how."

She nodded and opened her mouth to say more, but was cut off as the door slammed open, banging against the wall and causing it to creak worryingly. What was even more worrying, however, was the presence of Dejafosse, his broad frame filling the doorway. His beard quivered with tightly controlled anger, and he raised one thick finger to point at me, the other hand at his side, gripping his whip. Sacha stood and hurriedly scrambled away from the door, grabbing his sister's hand and pulling her to the back wall of the room, where they stood close together, their stances defensive.

"Now you've done it. I think I've been more than fair—more than *kind* to you boy, but that's all done now." I gulped and stood quickly, taking several steps forward so that I stood between the captain and the siblings. I strained my neck to look into the hall behind the captain, frowning as I saw that he was alone.

"Where's Octave?" I asked, hoping he couldn't hear the nervousness in my voice.

"Why? Worried he won't be here to save your neck again?" His mocking tone scratched at my nerves, but I kept quiet, trying to hold back my own temper. "He and I had a talk about you. It's one thing to steal from my men, but to steal from *me?* Are you a natural born idiot?"

"No," I replied. "I spent much of my early life studying to become this stupid." I heard Sacha snort behind me. Shaking my head, I held my hands out to him, palms up. "Besides, I have no idea what you're talking about."

He snarled, and I watched as flecks of spit got caught in the hair on his chin.

"You damn well know! My medicine. You think I can't tell when someone's been rooting through my personal possessions? I can tell. I can sure as hell tell! I don't know how you did it, but I'm not so easily fooled."

Sucking in my chest, I shook my head again, though meeker than before. "I don't know what medicine you're talking about. I'm not even sick."

I watched as his gaze slid from my face to the room behind me, and he lifted his left hand, pointing to the siblings with the handle of his whip. "Perhaps these two have had a bad influence on you. Shows you what happens when your only company is two worthless street rats."

"Oy! Now watch your mouth." I turned my head in time to see Sacha surging forward. I stumbled as he rammed into my side, apparently overwhelmed with his need to get to the captain. I flung out an arm to hold him back. "I don't need some sailor telling me how much I'm worth. I'll have you know I don't give a rat's arse about your opinion of me. Out of my way, Marin."

He jabbed his elbow into my rib cage, one hand coming down to my side to push me away, but I held fast. Twisting in his grip I grabbed his shoulders and shoved him backwards. His back hit the wall, and he stopped. I stood, fists clenched for a minute, waiting to see if he'd lunge again, but he did nothing. He merely folded his arms across his chest and glared at Dejafosse. Despite my extreme desire to see my accidental captor struck across the face by a boy, I knew that antagonizing a man like Dejafosse would cause more trouble than it was worth.

Meanwhile, Dejafosse seemed unperturbed by the outburst. He eyed Sacha dismissively, then returned his gaze to me.

"Enough of this, boy. I will give you one last chance to hand the medicine to me willingly. If you do so, your punishment may be less severe."

Gritting my teeth, I wondered why I was bothering to lie to the man. Perhaps in the vain hope that he might believe me and leave. Perhaps in the belief that as long as I held my tongue, he wouldn't be winning. "I didn't take your medicine."

He sighed and rubbed his temple. "All right, be that way. It will be seven lashes; now empty your pockets." I stood frozen and watched as a vein in his forehead became more prominent. "*Now,* boy, or it'll be ten."

I looked back at Sacha and Orpheline. Sacha had not moved; he stood with his arms crossed and his head still low to his chest. Orpheline, on the other hand, shifted her gaze between me and the captain, her face pale and her posture tense. She looked like she was worried, and the thought calmed me down a bit. Sticking my hands in my jacket pockets, I faced Dejafosse once more. Slowly, I turned out the pockets and, once receiving a nod as he deemed them empty, I removed my jacket to reveal my blouse underneath, which held no pockets. I stood waiting for him to say something.

"Your trouser pockets, too, boy." He raised an eyebrow and his lips curved up, as if he knew he had me beat. I didn't even breathe. I knew that the moment I pulled the bottle from my pants I would be dragged to the top deck for lashings. After that I would probably be subjected to the same conditions as Orpheline and Sacha, tin of coins or not. Swallowing my fear, I shoved my hand into my left pocket.

It was empty.

I froze, my eyes wide. I quickly put my right hand into the opposite pocket and felt around. Both were definitely empty.

"Well?" Dejafosse demanded, his tone impatient. "Turn your pockets out at once; let's have it."

Looking at him with what I hoped was a look of nonchalance, I pulled the fabric of my pockets out. His eyes grew to mirror mine, and he looked at me suspiciously.

"All right, so you're smart. Where've you hidden it then? Is it in the desk?"

I began to respond, but wasn't given the chance. "He hasn't got it, *sir.*" Both Dejafosse and I looked sharply at Sacha, and I nearly choked. He was leaning on the wall casually, one hand tucked into the pocket of his uniform coat, the other next to his face, the empty medicine bottle dangling between his thumb and forefinger.

Dejafosse spluttered for a moment before clearing his throat. "How could you have taken that?"

"Doesn't matter," Sacha replied easily. "Point is I've got it. My sister was sick. We've been down here in the cold and the wet, and her throat got sore. So I went out and took this. Wouldn't have had to if you'd given us better living quarters." He smiled in a wolfish way and twirled the bottle once. "Oh! And you should always make sure you lock this door securely before you leave. Really, Captain, you've no one to blame but yourself."

Orpheline was staring at her brother as if she could will him to stop talking. Or throttle him. I, on the other hand, was floored. The lazy sincerity with which Sacha spoke—*I* almost believed he'd stolen the medicine. He spoke again.

"Whip me, then. Won't matter; you're just going to have me hanged in a month or so, why bother with the wasted energy? To prove a point?"

Awkwardly, I stood between the two of them, gaping as Sacha spoke. The muscles in Dejafosse's jaw moved several times, his knuckles white around the whip. After several moments, he took a deep breath.

He said, "I've got more important things to do at the moment than to bother with you." He turned on his heel, moving to the door. Before he left, he placed his hand on the doorframe. "Sleep lightly, street rat; I'll be back for you." Without another word, he swept out, closing and locking the door behind him.

The hold was silent. I stared at Sacha. He looked back, an eyebrow raised bemusedly. Shaking my head, I raised a finger, jabbing him in the chest.

"You!" I cried.

He grinned. "You're welcome."

"You picked me!"

"Yes. Again, you're welcome."

"I can't believe you did that!"

"Hey, I just bumped into you. That bottle happened to fall into my hand. Really, neither of us is at fault here."

I continued to fume at him, and yet I found myself unable to stop a smile from creeping onto my face. The sheer absurdity of the situation was bubbling in my gut.

"I thought you were going to hit him!"

He shrugged, tossing the bottle from one hand to the other. "So did I. Turns out, I thought of a much better idea at the last second." We stared at each other, still thrilling with subsiding nerves.

"Why did you do that?" I asked quietly. He looked away under my gaze and rubbed his neck.

"Ah...I don't know." He chuckled, pocketing the bottle. "Let's call it returning a favor."

"You two are idiots," Orpheline chimed in from the corner. She was lying down, her head resting on a pile of hay.

She spoke sternly to her brother. "Especially you. You could have gotten yourself killed before we even reach land. You still may not make it. He said he's coming back for you."

"No, he just said that to scare me," Sacha replied with confidence. Even I rolled my eyes at that, and moved to the hay barrels, exhausted now that the adrenaline rush was over.

"Marin, wait." I paused and glanced at Orpheline.

"Something wrong?" I asked.

She shook her head. "No, nothing's wrong, it's just…" She rolled onto her back and stared up at the ceiling. She seemed to be having trouble finding the right words. "Look, if it hadn't been for my brother's move, you would be upstairs having your skin shredded right now." She let out a long breath and turned her head, looking at me with an open expression. "I know that you went to get the medicine for me, so…thank you."

I stood, my mouth agape. After a minute, she tutted, pursing her lips. "Well? Say something!"

"Your throat feels better."

She raised an eyebrow then laughed softly, a simple smile gracing her face. "Yes. Yes, it feels much better." She turned onto her side, facing away from me. "Goodnight, Marin."

I sat on the hay, curling in on myself slightly and pulling my jacket tight around my shoulders. I asked Sacha if he would show me the trick he had used on the captain, and he agreed. We stayed up late into the night and spoke in hushed voices about the journey, and our siblings and our homesickness.

He told me he actually, surprisingly, didn't mind my company and I told him he sounded disappointed. He just laughed and carried on teaching me the trick. I spent most of the night ignoring the flutter I had felt in my stomach as Orpheline had bid me goodnight.

Chapter Thirteen

The landing in Africa went about as smooth as one could hope. About an hour before we reached the port, the ship hit sudden, shallow water, and the rocking became something unbearable. I was called to the deck in order to help with the docking, seeing as two of the younger men had been found vomiting violently over the edge of the ship behind the goat pens. There was a moment of terrifying worry when the bottom of the ship scraped against a raised sand dune below the waves, and the captain called for a full halt. Octave said that when something like that happened, the best thing to do was to hope the waves carried you off the dune. He said that if you tried to force the ship off, it could damage the boat, which, with three months left before we'd arrive back in Calais, would cause us more harm than good.

We stayed marooned on the silt dune for over an hour, with the boat moving several inches every few minutes. What with all the shouting of the crew, and the constant tossing of the boat, it very well might have been the single most frustrating hour of my life. The rocking the collision caused was intense, and caused water to be knocked up onto the top deck and around the edges of the ship, causing seasickness in several of the animals. About half way off the dune, I ducked down to the hold to see how Sacha and Orpheline were doing, and to bring them a much-needed bucket for their troubles.

The breath of all the men caught when, for just a moment, one of the ropes holding the sails to the mast came undone, and it looked like we might lose it to the wind. By what I can only call sheer luck, the wind blew the rope my way, and as it struck me in the hip I grabbed it tight, yelling as I was dragged forward by the strength of it. I worried for a moment I might be thrown from the ship, but I felt a pair of hands covering my own, and I looked up to see Octave above me. He smiled at me, and I stared at him until he stopped smiling and rolled his eyes and shouted over the wind to start pulling the rope again. Together we managed to get the rope back to the mizzenmast and re-secure the sail. I wanted to thank him for forgiving me for my stupidity the week before. Instead, I just thanked him for his help with the sail and he chuckled, clapping me on the shoulder and assuring me that he regretted not letting the wind carry me off. My mood lifted considerably.

By the time the tide rolled in and lifted the ship off the dune the sky was darkening overhead and what land we could see in the distance was beginning to fade. We raised the sails and took off once more, and just as the first stars began to glint in the sky, Gérard called port from the crow's nest, and I was sent below again for the evening.

I slipped myself between Orpheline and Sacha where they sat against the back wall, silently. Remaining still for a few moments, I watched flecks of dust float from the ceiling as the men up top rushed around in their haste to get onto dry land.

Soon however, I became bored with the silence, and nudged Sacha roughly with my shoulder.

"Any reason you two aren't speaking?" No response, so I turned to Orpheline. "Phe, how's your day going then?"

She raised an eyebrow at me. "I've been stuck in here, and *don't* call me Phe."

"Fair enough," I replied, lazily dropping my head to my chest. I tried once more. "Did you two know it's the twenty sixth day of April tomorrow?"

"Your point is what?"

I gaped at her. "It's *Easter* tomorrow, you nutter! You mean to tell me you don't care for Easter?" No response. "You two are ridiculous; Easter is by far the best day of the year." Closing my eyes, I allowed my mind to drift back to Paris for a moment. "If I were at home right now, it would be splendid.

Just about this time of the day, my mother would be in the parlor, setting up chairs and tables for tomorrow's dinner. Oh, and *dinner*. Dinner tomorrow would be decadent. Our Betty would be in the kitchen, working over some herbs and lamb. I'd probably ask her for an Easter pastry, and she'd say no of course, but she'd still pretend not to see me when I came back later and took one anyway. Father would be out on his bedroom balcony, shouting to people walking below. Well…" I trailed off, fidgeting with the ends of my shirtsleeves, twisting the fabric between my fingers. "I suppose they won't be doing that this year, actually. I suppose they haven't done much at all since I left."

"Oh, God, will you stop whinging?" My eyes snapped open, at Sacha's sharp tone.

"I beg your pardon?"

"Are you really so pig-headed as to think that your entire family has just been sitting around weeping, or wandering the halls lost since you went left? You said they've got jobs, they've got lives. What do they do, anyway? Lick the king's boots for a living?"

I scowled at him. "I'll have you know they're hard-working people."

"Oh, please," he scoffed. "Nobody in the upper class is hard working."

"You are so incredibly prejudiced!" I shook my head at him in disbelief. "Both of my parents are tutors in the king's court. They educate children. My brother gathers information on surrounding countries and assists the cartographers in drawing maps for His Majesty's library. That's certainly more than you do in a day."

"There you go then!" Sacha exclaimed. "They've all got busy lives, your family. They've probably been getting on with them, and maybe in the back of their minds they hope you'll show up again one day if the wind is right, but let's be honest—they've got more important things to worry about than where you are now."

The room was tense. I didn't know whether to yell at Sacha or hit him. What did *he* know about my family? What did he know about not having parents when you need them?

Probably more than you do, a voice in my head replied. I felt my throat beginning to close, and I swallowed thickly. Sacha and Orpheline suddenly felt much too close to me and the room felt far too warm. My eyes stinging, I struggled to my feet.

"Marin, he didn't mean—" Orpheline began, but I cut her off before she could finish.

"He meant what he meant. It doesn't matter; I don't care either way." I tried to laugh, but it sounded forced to my ears. I shoved my hands in my pockets and clenched them to stop them shaking. I kept picturing my family at home now, curled up in front of a fire, smiling and laughing as if it didn't matter that I wasn't there. As if they didn't miss me at all. As if—

"Let's read it."

I frowned at Sacha. Orpheline frowned, too. He shrugged and rubbed the back of his neck, scratching the short hairs there. "Phe is right. That wasn't fair of me to say, and…well…I don't want you throwing a fit or anything so if you want to…all right. Let's read the diary." As he spoke, he pulled the leather journal from inside his coat and tossed it onto the floor at my feet.

I no longer felt like breaking down. I no longer felt like yelling. I no longer felt like doing anything at all in the whole world except opening that journal. I heard Orpheline whisper to Sacha, "You sure?" and he nodded before waving his hand at me quickly.

"Well, go on then, magic hands, open it. Happy Easter."

I grinned widely and dropped to my knees, reaching into my hair and pulling out the pins. Fingers itching with excitement, I slotted the metal easily into the small iron lock and began to twist and press them. As the bottom lock found its niche, I began to lean in, vaguely marveling over the fact that I was finally going to see what was inside. After several minutes, the top pin clicked into place and the lock jolted out of position. I looked up at the siblings excitedly, and they smiled back. They seemed nervous. I wished I could reassure them that nothing was going to hurt them because we read this journal. I wouldn't let anything hurt them over some silly diary.

With slightly shaky and newly calloused fingers I pulled the lock loose and turned the book onto its spine. With one last deep breath I opened the journal to the center page and gazed down.

Allies in Foreign Ports:
Silvestre Touchet
Roche Chauvin
Arluin Begnoche
Lucien Paradis

I blinked slowly and tried to process what I was seeing. I handed the journal to Sacha, and he just shook his head and shrugged. I looked at it once more. *These names…these allies…allies? What allies?* I thought to myself. *The King's allies? These are French men, I should know these men. I've had dinner with the king's men. I don't understand."*

I turned to another page and more names jumped out at me. Men and women and titles…each page had a header. *Paris Housing in State of Distress…Meeting Point for Post Leave…In City Weaponry…Point of Barricades…Discussion House—La Chaloupe…*

"It's a rebellion," I whispered. Orpheline cursed next to me, and I looked up at her. "That's what this is. This is the beginning of a *rebellion.* Surely you've heard rumors in the city that one is starting?" I stared in shock at the pages, before freezing to think for a moment.

This was an opportunity. I had fallen out of Dejafosse's good grace that was for sure. This would get me back into his good book. I'd get a room up above. Hell, I'd get *his* room if I wanted, with information like this! It went further than that even—I could bring this to the king. Imagine how he would repay me! I had never been as smart as my brother. Never as good at maths or Latin. With one brother already on course for the King's Court, I would need more than my natural abilities—which weren't much—in order to win a place with the court as well. This was a ticket for me. And not just for me—for Sacha and Orpheline too! I would love to see anyone try to put them in jail once they'd turned this book over to the court. Impossible. They would go from thieves to nobility over night. We could achieve that together. I told them as much.

"That's enough reading," Orpheline snapped, pulling the book from me mid-turn.

"I've not read them all yet," I told her. "There's got to be a hundred more names in that book."

She passed the book to her brother who put it under his jacket again. "Look, Marin," she began softly. "I know you're trying to help—yourself, as well as us—but this has gone too far. It's too dangerous already."

I shook my head emphatically. "You don't understand! The danger disappears the moment we turn this journal in. The moment it's in the king's hands, we're all free. We're all *royalty*."

Sacha was smiling a little, though he tried to hide it in his coat collar. Orpheline look unconvinced.

"I know that you're excited, Marin, but it's too much of a—"

"Risk? Not at all! We'll go give it to the captain. He'll invite us to dinner in his quarters, just watch. We'll be strolling around the royal gardens by Christmas."

"Marin, I really don't think that—"

"All right, let's do it." Orpheline and I turned to look at Sacha, who had stopped smiling and was now sitting up straight, looking pensive. I grinned and scooted closer to him.

"Brilliant. I'll go knock on the door. Octave will hear it and come down and then we'll tell him we have urgent news for the Captain."

Orpheline was still staring, a shocked expression on her face, at her brother. Sacha shook his head slightly. "No, Marin, we're not taking it to Dejafosse."

"But you said—"

"I said we can take it to the king. We will. First moment we step off the ship we'll announce that we've got the journal. Then we have to show it to the king, but as long as we can make it to him, I'm willing to give this up." He glanced sideways at Orpheline. "For king and country and all that."

I nodded slowly, his thinking almost making sense. "Why can't we show it to Dejafosse? I know he's a snake, of course, but he'd treat us better if we were to give him this."

"You think he'd let us have it?" Orpheline piped up, moving over to sit next to her brother. "The moment we show it to him, he'll turn the ship around and head back to France. We can't forget Pondicherry."

"Why not?" I asked, not caring about the trip as much as I previously had.

"Because…those guns are for our King! It can't be our fault that he doesn't receive them." Sacha chimed in. "She's right. Besides, like she said, Dejafosse would never let us take the credit for the journal. He'd say he caught it on us, took it from us as he daringly captured us or some drivel like that." He began to get more excited. "He'd try to pin it on us. He'd probably try to say it was *our* journal! That we were in with the revolution or something!"

"Sacha," Orpheline snapped, glaring at him. "Don't talk like that, you'll tempt fate."

He rolled his eyes but wilted all the same. "All right, all right, calm down." He looked back at me and stuck out a dirty hand. "We'll hand over this journal to His Majesty, the great and terrible King Prat, when and *only when*…we get back to France. Deal?"

I looked down at his palm for just a moment, before deciding that the eventually glory would surely surpass the immediate reward. I grinned, and thrust my hand into his.

"Deal."

Chapter Fourteen

It took us more than an hour to load the guns aboard the *Tromperie.* It took us more than *two* hours to load the General aboard.

"You be careful with those, you hear me? Can't have your clumsiness setting off a rifle!" He scuttled frantically over the top deck, his white hair pulled back into a slick ponytail down his neck. He pointed with delicate hands as he directed the sailors where to place the guns. In return, the men eyed him like he was a dead squid that had washed up on deck. Métivier, his arms full of pouches of gunpowder, sidled past me, leaning down to nudge my shoulder with his elbow.

"'Ey, let's draw straws," he joked. "See who gets to throw him off the ship."

"You! Boy with spots, less talking, more carrying." Métivier glanced over his shoulder and nodded at the General, before turning back to me and gagging quietly under his breath. I laughed a bit louder than was probably appropriate. That was my mistake.

"You, dirty one, if you're not helping, you're in the way."

I froze and cursed softly before stepping forward toward the general. "Aye, sir, my mistake. Is there something I can help you with?"

He looked at me down his thin nose and curled his lip. "With arms that skinny you're hardly good for carrying anything. Montave! Is this boy yours?" I followed his eyes to Octave, who stood several feet away, leaning on one of the masts. His arms were folded tightly across his chest and a muscle in his forehead twitched slightly.

"No, General, I assure you he is not mine."

"Well, then, Montave," the general said, "can you at least find something to keep him busy?"

I laughed and tried to turn it into a sneeze in the sleeve of my jacket. Octave glared at me. "Yes, Montave," I said pleasantly, smiling at him. "Surely you can find something for me to do. Perhaps scrubbing up below deck?"

He cracked his neck and grinned down at me, his snaggled tooth glinting slightly in the sun. "Oh no, Marin, you've been so helpful today. I think I'll give you a pleasant job. Oh!" He snapped two thick fingers together. "I've got it. Why don't you assist the general here with any of his needs? Yes, you two should work well together."

The general placed a finger over his lips and hummed lightly, as if thinking over the offer. Behind him, I began shaking my head adamantly. Octave simply smiled sweetly back.

The general finally nodded. He said, "I suppose that will work well. Come on then, boy, you can come assist me in unpacking!" I followed reluctantly behind him as we went below, biting my thumb at Octave as we went.

We soon found ourselves in front of the physician's quarters. I looked at the general. "What are we doing here?"

"These are my rooms."

"These are the medic's rooms."

"Oh no, he's staying with the rest of the men for the duration of the trip. He's been so kind as to let me use these rooms! Or the captain's been so kind. Come on, boy."

He opened the door with a small brass key before slipping inside. I followed him in, standing patiently as he slipped the key onto a thin piece of rope that he placed around his neck.

"Now, those books," he began, pointing a spindly finger at a pile sitting atop a leather travelling case in the corner. "Those are very important records. They have the full inventory of my trip in them, and other personals. I trust you won't be so incompetent as to get them out of order or..." his lips twisted in disgust, "*smudge* them."

I raised an eyebrow and looked down at my hands. I was actually surprised to see them fairly dirty and blackened, no doubt from helping carry all the loads of gunpowder on board. Before coming on this ship, I couldn't once remember having dirty hands. My mother wouldn't have let me into the house if I had.

"Take those papers then and place them on the shelf against the wall."

I nodded vaguely and moved to the papers. As I began to set them upon the dresser, which only yesterday held bottles of medicine and remedies, I looked closer at the words written on the papers. They spoke of past ports where these guns had been stowed or transferred hands; inspectors who attested for the quality of the arms; the forms stating the maker of the weapons. All the papers had gone through many hands and many men, and all of them had recently been signed off by General A. Begnoche himself. Sheets of paper titled *"Destination of Goods"* and *"Contacts in Paris"* and a black rolled up scroll with the words written in white, the first letter of each word in gold; *"Letters Entreated of France"*.

"Oh, *damn you!"* the general spit. I looked at him, only to see him glaring down at his ring finger.

"Are you all right, sir?" I asked.

"Some wood has splintered in my finger. These damn ships would be fine if they weren't made out of wood. Why can't they be made out of glass, or copper or such?"

I looked back down at the papers and frowned. Something felt off. "I suppose it would make floating significantly harder, sir," I replied quietly. I flipped through the papers once more and chewed at my lip. I couldn't figure out what was nagging at me. "Where were you last staying, sir?" I asked.

"What?" He looked up from his finger, as if confused that I was talking to him. Finally he waved his un-injured hand at me. "Cape Colony, of course. Why?"

I shook my head. "No reason." I skimmed the pages twice more before giving up and placing the papers on the dresser. I listened to Begnoche groan again before rolling my eyes and reaching into my hair, pulling out one of the pins. I turned to him and knelt down, grabbing his hands. He made a noise just short of squealing and attempted to tug his hand away from me.

"What are you doing, you tiny *brute*?"

I chose to ignore him, and instead uncurled his finger from his palm and placed the tip of my pin to it, pressing in. It took less than ten seconds to get the splinter out, and I wiped the small drop of blood away with my thumb. I stood and brushed the dust off my knees. The general blinked at me, his cheeks pinking slightly.

"Is there anything else I can do for you, sir?"

He cleared his throat. "No, no, that will be all. You may go." I turned to leave, opening the door. I had one foot out when he called to me. "Oh! Go down to the kitchens now and tell the cook that *General Begnoche* is quite hungry and would love his food ready as soon as possible."

He spoke his own name with so much gusto that I pictured a bird, puffing up its feathers. I nodded without looking back and stepped out of the room, closing the door behind me. I began to walk down the hall and toward the galley. The nagging feeling persisted, and I rubbed my temples, trying to figure out where my unease was coming from. I walked into the galley and toward the cook, who was resting his short leg upon a chair and stirring some unidentifiable liquid in the pot. He glanced at me before looking back to his concoction.

"Aye?" He asked shortly.

"The general wants his food soon."

He eyed me suspiciously. "What general?"

"The general that's on the ship."

"I ain't heard'a any general on the ship," he said, turning his head and spitting into a copper pot. I scrunched up my nose.

"Well, perhaps if you talked to anyone you would know. General Begnoche wants his food ready soon, and God help you if you don't get it for him. He's a chore of a man."

"Well, tell General Beignet that he'll get his food when the rest'a the men do."

"*Begnoche*," I corrected him. "General A. Begno—" I froze. The thoughts in my head began to line up. The cook stared at me but I couldn't bring myself to move.

"You all right, sonny?"

"Begnoche," I whispered. I felt as if I'd been hit in the gut, all the air knocked out me. "A. Begnoche. General *A. Begnoche*." I spun on my heel and dashed from the galley. I needed to get to Octave, to get him to let me back into the hold. So I could tell Orpheline and Sacha about the general. So I could tell them his name. So I could tell them that I figured out what was bothering me about him. That I recognized his name and that I *knew* where I recognized him from.

His name was in the stolen journal.

Chapter Fifteen

"Are you sure you're right, Marin? There could be a dozen A. Begnoches in the world!"

"Yeah, and if you're wrong you'll be strung up by your toes—or worse."

I groaned and cupped my face in my hands for what felt like the tenth time that conversation. Pinching the bridge of my nose, I took a deep breath. "Yes. Yes, I am sure. It's…a gut feeling, I suppose. It has to be him, it's too much of a coincidence, don't you think? That he should happen to be on this boat, which left the port where you found *this journal?*" I shook my head. "No, it's certainly him. Besides, you didn't see him." I snorted, pulling my jacket tight around me as a gust of wind blew through the room. "The man's a complete ponce; of course he'd be working with the rebellion."

Sacha grimaced. Orpheline remained unchanged.

"Too risky. You can't prove it. You'll just get yourself hurt."

I laughed. "Oh right, and you don't want to see that."

The room suddenly crackled with tension, and I bit my tongue. I watched apprehensively as Orpheline's face turned a bright pink, her teeth clenched tight. She stood up.

"No. As hard as it may be for your pea-sized brain to understand, I actually would *not* want that to happen." She walked the short distance to the corner and slumped down, tucking her head into her arms. "I'm going to sleep. First boy who wakes me gets scalped."

I looked at Sacha, who shook his head and tutted at me. Even though I knew he was mostly joking, it still felt bad to see. I tipped my head back until it thudded against the wall painfully. Sacha chuckled and threw his arm around my shoulder.

"You've got to work on your way with words, my friend."

***

"How do you like the General?"

I stared incredulously at Octave. He laughed. "Come on, boy, he's not *too* bad."

We were up above the top deck, sitting on the top yard of the mizzenmast, securing the rigging to the topsail. The skies were gray and deeply clouded, and the tops of the masts were stark against the heavens. I closed my eyes, sucked in deep breaths of stone cold air, and let it fill my chest. Opening one eye, I looked at Octave.

"Well, fine, *Montave,* if you like him then you can spend tonight listening to him practice his thank you speech to the king for an hour." I smiled grimly as Octave laughed, but the anxious churning in my gut grew. It had been three days since Begnoche arrived, and I'd yet to get Orpheline and Sacha's blessing to turn in the general. They were still holding fast to "no evidence, no accusations." On the one hand, they had a point. If I couldn't prove that Begnoche was a mole—if I couldn't find any solid evidence that condemned him—I'd be setting myself up for arrest.

"Are your ears even workin' today, boy?"

I blinked at Octave. "What? Sorry I...what?"

"I asked you to pass me a last bit of the rigging. What's on your mind today? You're not in the right place."

Begnoche was on the tip of my tongue. I bit it quiet.

"Nothing. I suppose I'm just worn down from dealing with the general." He laughed, and I took a deep breath, passing over the last bit of rope to him. "It's just...I wonder sometimes how you're supposed to trust or respect people who you just...*know* don't deserve that respect. Do you understand?"

He looked pensively at me for a moment, before turning to the rigging and tugging on it a few times to make sure it was secure. Nodding approvingly, he gripped my shoulder firmly.

"Come, sit with me." He pulled me carefully off the rigging until we stood precariously upon the top yard. We sat slowly and stared out across the hull of the ship into the distance, where the sun was creeping steadily toward the water. I drifted into my own thoughts until his voice broke my reverie. "When I first began sailing, I had a captain I didn't think much of. Not much of at all. To be honest, I thought he was a right arse. I wouldn't listen to a damn word he said." I watched patiently, as with calloused hands he reached up and scratched at his scraggly chin.

"Did he turn out to be a ponce?"

He barked out a laugh. "Course he did! He especially was to me, 'cause he didn't want me on board to begin with. He tried to get rid o' me once or twice. But he *also* turned out to be the one of the best Captains I've ever seen. Him and Dejafosse."

"Dejafosse? *He's* your idea of a good captain?"

"Great one. Just like his father," he said.

I paused. "His father…wait, his father your first captain?"

"The very same."

"The last captain of this ship?"

"Aye." I gaped at him. "Oy, close your mouth." He stretched a hand out and batted the side of my face with his palm. "What're you staring at, boy?"

"*You were the stowaway,*" I whispered. He spluttered, his cheeks darkening.

"Wh-who told you that nonsense? I never—" He paused and groaned, shaking his head. He looked out at the water and chuckled deeply. "Ah, damn. I should have expected this when I stuck you in a room with Deole. He'd be the only one old enough on this ship to even remember that. I'm right, am I?" He looked to me, and I nodded sheepishly, fiddling with my fingers.

My legs dangled over the wooden pole, and I thought about how, just several months ago, I had been so scared of the idea of spending so long a time on a ship. Scared of having to climb these heights, and talk to these men, and sail these seas. Now, three months later, the ship was the least of my worries. Treason was occurring below me, and I was the only one who could do anything—and I was doing nothing.

"He's not as bad as you think." I looked up as Octave spoke suddenly. I frowned.

"Who, Deole?"

"No, not Deole, you twit. The captain." He exhaled heavily and hit his hand against his knee lightly, the brown fabric of his trousers scratching at the back of his hand until it turned red. "I know you're upset because he keeps your...friends, down in holding, but really, it is their own fault. They're not even smart criminals. Who hides in the hole with the extra rigging? That's the first place someone would look for a stowaway. Much better places to hide. Take the crawl space behind the orlop. It stays warm seein' as it's just behind the capstan, and it's close enough to the galleys to allow you get food with little incident. On top of that, it's accessible from the outside of the ship. If you can stand the stench of sick sailors, it's practically homey!" I made a weak attempt to laugh, but it came out as a scoff. He sighed and put his hand back on my shoulder. "You have to understand that they don't mean no good to us. They're thieves, and it's Captain Dejafosse's job to do something about them."

I shook my head vehemently. "You're wrong. They...yes, all right they're thieves. Is that their fault, though?" I looked out in front of me, squinting against the sun as it peeked out behind the billowing sails. "Perhaps they are not the criminals. Perhaps the criminals are the ones who have put them in a situation where they must steal to live."

I felt more than saw Octave's weary look. "That person would be the king, boy. Surely you're not..."

"What? No! Of course I don't blame the king..." *Who do you blame?* "That makes it sound like..."

"Treason?" he supplied.

"Exactly. Which I, of course, am against. Fully." I paused. *Take this opportunity,* a voice in my head shouted. "If one happened to know of any thing of that sort—the treason sort, that is—say they knew something like that was happening, or going happen, it would be their moral duty, to king, country— God, really—to tell someone about it...right?"

Octave stared down at me, his blue eyes flickering between my own brown ones. "What are you asking, Marin?"

I took a deep breath. "Octave, I really think you should tell the Captain to gather all the men to top deck."

**

The sky was beginning to darken into night when Octave hurried all the men top deck. They stood in lines, just as they had that day I had almost been flayed. Octave and I, once more, stood side by side in front of Dejafosse's cabin doors. A shiver ran through me, and I prayed that this time would not end in a successful whipping from the captain.

He eventually—after what seemed like years—stepped out of his cabin, Begnoche at his side. The two were smiling jovially, and I swallowed. This would be much easier if Dejafosse disliked Begnoche as much as the rest of us did. It would be harder if they were chummy. As Dejafosse spotted me he let out a groan of annoyance, eyeing me with distaste.

"Octave, when you said you needed my utmost attention, I didn't think it would be for something so trivial. I told you to handle all dealings with this boy from here on out."

"Aye, Captain," Octave said politely. "He assures me this is important, however, and that you personally will want to hear this." His hand, resting on my shoulder, squeezed in support. "Marin, go ahead."

I took a slow step forward and, gathering my courage, looked the captain dead in the eye and spoke.

"There is a traitor to the king on board the *Dame Tromperie.*" Immediately, hushed whispers burst out among the men, and I watched with slight satisfaction as Begnoche's eyes widened a fraction. Dejafosse clenched his fists.

"Who among my men, *boy,*" he spat viciously, "would you dare accuse of treason?"

"None of them," I said, trying to ignore the way my voice cracked. "The one I accuse is no man of yours." I looked over at Octave who was looking at me with wide eyes, his face pale. I wondered if he thought I was lying. If so, I would be hanged. I wondered if he was scared of that happening. Sucking in a shaky breath, I turned forward again, my eyes slipping from the captain to the general. "The one I accuse...is General Begnoche."

The men were positively buzzing now. Beside me, Octave had closed his eyes, as if he wished this moment would stop, yet his grip on my shoulder stayed firm. The captain looked between the two of us and Begnoche, looking for any reaction.

"QUIET!" he roared, his voice silencing the men. "I don't know what you're playing at anymore, boy, but it ends now."

I looked around, catching sight of various men as they watched the scene play out. I felt myself sweating, thinking that perhaps Sacha and Orpheline's warnings should have been taken a bit more seriously. "I swear to you, I'm telling the truth. This man is a traitor to the throne! He means to assist a rebellion! Surely you've heard rumors of one starting in the city?"

Begnoche's face turned a deep red, and I stood nervous but determined as his glare deepened. He turned to the captain. "Please, this is ridiculous! What proof does this boy have?"

I swallowed, but would not be deterred. "I have...his rooms! Search them, I'm sure you'll find something you need, something to prove this!" It sounded far-fetched in my ears, and I could tell I wasn't convincing the captain.

"That is enough!" Dejafosse shouted. "This has gone too far. You cannot accuse a respected man, with years of service to the throne, of *treason*!" He looked to the crew. "Octave, you've clearly been swayed by this boy. We'll have to do without your help then. Métivier—tie the boy up."

Looking at me apologetically, Octave stepped forward and, with a survival instinct I hadn't been aware that I had, I lunged forward, not thinking, my hand shooting out toward Begnoche's neck. Ignoring the general's high-pitched shriek of "My God! The boy means to kill me!" I grabbed the rope and key and pulled, ripping it from him and dashing down the deck, slipping beneath the arms of the men.

Flinging the door to the lower decks open, I barreled down the stairs and began to sprint down the halls, toward the medic's cabin, the shouts of the men echoing in my ears. I reached the door of Begnoche's cabin and shoved the key into the lock, yanking the door open. Closing it behind me and locking it once more, I froze.

What in God's good name was I doing? I had no idea what I was looking for. Even if I did, why did I think that the general would be so foolish as to leave incriminating material around his rooms? My chest heaved, and I shook with adrenaline, my eyes landing on the leather travelling case. I threw it open and fell to my knees before it.

"Get him out! You keep that heathen from my room!"

The men gathered outside the room as I began tossing aside used handkerchiefs and bottles of congestion medicine. I was hoping for proof, *praying* that I wasn't wrong.

"One last chance to come out, boy, before I rip your teeth out!" I didn't respond. I moved to the desk and began pulling the drawers open. "Deole! Somebody get Deole to the front and have him open this damn door!" The drawers were filled with lint and bugs and blouses and what appeared to be a spare wig and none of it was worth anything. I heard Deole's drawl from outside the door and the click of pins in the lock. Deole had taught me. Surely he'd be in here in less than a minute, and I *couldn't find anything.*

"What is taking so long?"

"I'm sorry, sir, it's my old bones, they just don't work like they used to."

I tugged at my hair, my breath quickening as I realized that this could be it. I might have failed. In a last ditch effort, I reached for the papers on the desk, shuffling through them.

"What is taking this man so long, Captain? I thought he was your best." Begnoche was hissing.

"He. Is. Supposed. To. Be." Dejafosse replied through gritted teeth, his voice muffled behind the wood door.

My eyes skimmed familiar titles, of no consequence. *Receipt of Purchase, Time Log of Port Departures, Letters Entreated of France, Map of Past Route—*

I went back. *Letters Entreated of France,* on a black scroll with the first letter of each word scrawled in bright gold letters: *L.E.F.* This was it. I grabbed it, and as I heard Deole's voice calmly saying, "Sir, I may have ta get better tools for this," I sprang up and unlocked the door, swinging it open and closing my eyes. I shoved out the hand holding the scroll out.

"Read this."

The men fell into a hush, and I felt the scroll being pulled from my trembling fingers. I kept my eyes clenched, too scared that at any moment I might feel the sting of a whip or hear the blast of a gun. Instead, I heard the rustle of parchment being unfurled.

"Sir, you...you need to read this." Octave's voice was more hesitant than I'd ever heard it, and I opened my eyes, blinking as they adjusted. Octave, Deole, Dejafosse, and Begnoche stood before the door; behind them, the rest of the men were attempting to get close enough to hear what was being said. Dejafosse had a hand raised, most likely to hit me, but he lowered it long enough to snatch the open scroll from Octave. Begnoche stood by, and I watched him squirm, as if debating whether it would be better or worse for him to make a grab for the scroll.

Dejafosse's eyes skimmed the surface of the paper, and I watched, with growing excitement, as they widened. Finally, he lifted his eyes from the paper to stare at me. I smiled, my terror fading away into sheer joy. He jabbed a finger into my chest.

"*You.*" I flinched, only to feel his hand coming up to clasp around my shoulder. "You come with me. Octave, keep this *general* here until I come back."

The captain and I walked together toward the stairs out of the hold. I moved to go up them, but was tugged back by my collar. I followed, confused, as Dejafosse led me into a part of the ship I had been in only once before. The men trailed behind us as we went. We all ended up in a room somewhere in the middle of the ship. The air was warm and muggy and felt nothing like the chill outside. It was larger than the galley or the hold, but seemed small due to the plethora of hammocks strung from the ceiling: seven rows of five, with two hammocks in one place, one lower to the floor and one just a bit off of the floor.

"Sir?"

"Welcome," he said, "to the crew's sleeping quarters." He sniffed through his nose, before nodding as if pleased with himself. He snapped, "Métivier! Which bunk is yours?"

Métivier scurried into the room and stood beside a hammock near the back of the room, which hung low to the floor and was covered with an assortment of thin blankets. He grinned. "This'un, sir."

"Right, good." Dejafosse turned to me, and jerked his thumb behind him toward Métivier. "There's your new bunk, boy. You'll get your new assignments in the morning."

Métivier and I gaped at him—Métivier most likely in anger, and me from shock.

"My...my bunk?"

"You're a crew member. Crew members sleep in with the crew."

I spluttered for a moment before grinning in disbelief. "I'm a crew member now?"

He raised an eyebrow. "You didn't think you could do something like that and not get promoted, did'ya?" He winked and turned around, heading toward the door. "To bed boys, you're up early in the morning." He turned at the door, snuffing out the candles by the doorway. The other men began getting into their hammocks. I piped up before he could walk out the door.

"Goodnight, sir."

He turned back to me and smirked. "You've been a pain every minute of this trip until today. I hope that's changing now. Get your sleep, Marin L'Émule. You're playing with the big boys now."

The door closed tight behind him. As I got in the hammock and stared up at the back of another sailor and listened to Métivier grumble in the corner and felt a cool breeze drift across my face, I wondered how Sacha and Orpheline were down in the hold.

I wondered if I wouldn't be happier down there with them.

Chapter Sixteen

My new tasks were as follows: Checking the rigging on the masts before breakfast; taking over Begnoche's position and manning the guns in their storage throughout the day, including cleaning and oiling them and making sure they were all still there; bringing food and water down to Sacha and a very irate Orpheline.

"Where were you last night?" Orpheline asked, materializing in front of me as I closed the door. "Were you with Dejafosse? Did he do anything to you? Oh, come *here,* you stupid boy." She began to look me over frantically, and I was uncomfortably reminded of the way my mother would behave whenever I'd come back from playing with the other boys. I placed my hands on her shoulders and shook her lightly.

"*Phe,* I'm fine. More than fine, I have wonderful news!"

Sacha cocked an eyebrow at me from where he sat. "Good news? What, did you stay out in the rain all night and catch a case of the flu?"

"Why would I consider that good news?"

"Because dying would be preferable to spending another day down here," he joked. I grinned at him.

"Funny you should say that…I won't be spending any more time down here."

Orpheline stared blankly at me, and Sacha exclaimed "My God, the captain's going to kill you today, isn't he?"

"No," I said, walking over to him and sitting next to him against the wall. "I've been offered a hammock."

"No, you haven't," Orpheline said slowly. "Hammocks are for crew."

I nodded, shrugging. "Right you are."

"What are you saying?" Sacha asked, his face a mask of trepidation. "That you're on the crew now?" I nodded again. I slid my hand down between the two of us, slipping it into his pocket. "Oh yeah? And how'd you manage to pull that off?"

The string tied around my finger, I let the bandalore dip to the floor. Sacha's eyes widened, and he made a grab for it, but I pulled it just out of reach, laughing. "I'm getting good at this!" I whooped as he punched me in the arm, snatching his toy back.

"Don't be a child, Marin."

"After you, good *sir.*"

"BOYS."

Sacha and I jumped at Orpheline's shout, and I stared at her. "What?"

"Perhaps we can spend less time talking about *toys* and more time explaining why on earth you're now a member of the crew, hmm?"

"Let's just say I gave them some valuable information." I smirked. What happened next was more terrifying than all the death threats I had received on the ship so far. Orpheline's face grew dark, her hair falling in front of her eyes. Her hands clenched at her sides and beside me Sacha tensed. In the next second I was pulled up from my spot on the ground and slammed against the wall, Orpheline's hands tight around my collar and the rough wood of the wall scratching and digging into my back. I choked slightly as the pressure on my throat increased.

"*What. Did. You. Tell. Them?*" I shook my head at her. Below me, Sacha was tugging at my pants leg.

"I'd tell her, Marin, before she takes an eye out."

"All right, all *right!*" I grabbed her wrists, trying to pull them off my throat, but too scared of what she might do if I tried to shove her back. "I didn't tell them about the journal, I swear!" Her hold loosened, and I sucked in a much-needed breath. "I told them about Begnoche."

"Why would you do that?"

"Because he's trying to betray the king, and I knew that I could prove it."

"What proof did you have?"

I grinned sheepishly. "I took a chance, and it paid off. He had some sort of incriminating evidence—a scroll, with the same initials as the journal. L, E, F." I took advantage of her loose fingers and pried her hands off of me. "Smart, don't you think?"

"I think not," she replied. She took a step back and ran a hand over her face. I noted with worry that she wouldn't look me in the eye. "You're sure you didn't tell them about the journal?"

I moved toward her and clasped her elbow lightly. "I didn't. I wouldn't." I looked at Sacha, whose eyes were wide and his face flushed slightly. "Look, I know you two need that journal as your collateral for freedom, and I won't waste that. I promised, remember?"

They waited a beat, before Orpheline finally nodded, her face softening. "Fine, yes, all right." She rubbed her palms against her skirt, puffing air into her bangs, blowing them out of her eyes. "You should go, shouldn't you? Lots of official crew work to do."

"Yeah," Sacha said, stretching his arms above his head. "What do sailors do anyway? Besides lock up children?"

"Well, they go have dinner with the rest of the crew at sunset," I replied. "You two are actually one of my chores now."

"How sweet."

"You know what I mean. Water and food and whatnot."

"You're not going to make us answer questions for it this time, are you?"

I laughed, clearing my throat. "No, no I'm not." I chewed on my lip nervously. "I did have another idea, though." Orpheline moved to speak but I sped forward. "Just hear me out. We found one traitor on board. One traitor who we wouldn't have found…without the journal."

"Marin, I know where you're—"

"What if there are more? What if a whole group of rebels are on board, and their names are *all in this journal?* We could find them, turn them in—help the king! Imagine how big this could become?"

Orpheline was shaking her head, chewing on her thumbnail. "No, Marin."

"I don't think you understand. We'd be heroes!"

"This is not how you become heroes, Marin." Sacha said quietly. "Not like this.

I didn't understand. "We'd be helping the king."

"The answer is no, Marin."

"Think about the—"

"*No*, Marin."

"But what if we could—"

"ENOUGH," Sacha snapped. His face was red and his shoulders hunched. "We've said no, Marin. The journal is ours; we got it ourselves. You want it...you take it like we did." He slipped his hand down to his boot and whipped out his handmade dagger. I stared at it tensely, before chuckling.

"Oh really? I call your bluff. You're not going to use that against me."

"Maybe he will," Orpheline said grimly. "Don't test him."

I stared at her in disbelief. "I can't believe you two would be so selfish as to refuse this opportunity. Dejafosse didn't take the credit, he didn't accuse me of anything, why should he do any different to you?"

"We don't have a rich mummy and daddy, that's why," Orpheline snapped. "Forget about it. Go join your fellow men. I hope you enjoy the sailor's life."

"Phe, just listen to me, please."

"None of this changes the fact that we shook on it," Sacha said. "We made a deal, and you may want to back out of it, but I won't. Go finish your chores, sailor."

For a minute, I didn't move. I just stood there, tense, hoping one of them would say something. My chest was aching oddly, and I realized I didn't want this. I didn't want to be fighting with these two. I didn't want to be fighting with my *friends*. I nodded finally and stepped back.

"All right. I'll go. I'm not mad, so you know." Orpheline was still breathing heavily and Sacha still had his knife out and I was struck by the fact that they had spent their whole lives developing those defenses. "I'm not mad, but I think you're wrong. I think you'll realize you're wrong, and that no matter what the king has done, you both still want to help your country." Orpheline scoffed. "So I'll leave, but I'll be back tomorrow. Goodnight."

With that I turned away and left quietly. I stood outside the room, leaning on the closed door, hoping one of them might call my name. When neither did, I pushed off the wall and headed down to the gunroom to check on the weapons.

∗∗∗

"Sleep well, men," Dejafosse said as he stood in the doorway. "We arrive in Pondicherry in two days. Get your rest before we have to unload." He paused and peered at me in the dim light. "Marin."

"Aye, captain?"

"You did well today. I trust you'll do as well on the way back."

I nodded, smiling. "I'll do my best, sir."

He looked uncomfortable for a moment before straightening his shoulders and walking over to me. He lowered his voice so only I could hear and said, "I know you've mentioned the king's Court once or twice, but I…" He cleared his throat. "I should tell you that you've more than earned a place on this ship. If you find you can't keep yourself out of trouble on dry land," he joked.

I laughed awkwardly and shrugged my shoulders. "With my luck, I'd probably end up back on here thinking it was the carriage to Paris or something."

"Do you mean to say," he said, his beard curving around his grin, "that you'll think over the offer?"

"Captain?" Octave had appeared in the doorway. "The prisoner has finished his last requests. Would you like to hear them now or in the morning?"

Dejafosse shook his head. "Let's get it over with now, shall we?" He nodded to me once more before sweeping out of the room, calling "Night all" over his shoulder as he left.

I had to wait almost an hour before the rest of the men stopped talking about Indian women. Once the whispers and whistles died out, I slipped off my hammock, bare feet hitting the floor silently. Moving low to the ground, I left the room quickly, pulling a candlestick from the wall as I passed the doorway, and began my short journey to the hold. As I reached the door, I pulled the chain around my neck out from under my shirt. It was a tad heavy, with both the key to the gunroom and the key to the hold dangling from it now. Inserting the key, I cursed silently. Wrong key. They looked exactly alike. Switching them quickly I unlocked the door quietly as I could and hurried inside, closing it behind me. I froze as the door creaked into place and Orpheline groaned in her sleep, rolling over. Letting out a sigh of relief as she stayed asleep, I placed the candlestick in one of the mantles by the door, and moved across the room on my toes, kneeling down when I reached Sacha.

In that moment, I tried to remember all the tips of theft that these two had taught me.

Step number one: Make sure your mark is distracted; sleep was a distraction.

Step two: Put pressure on a part of their body that they aren't protecting—if somebody is hiding something on their body, say a journal, they'll be especially sensitive if that place is touched. So put more pressure on a part of them that they aren't guarding. Keeping this in mind, I rested my left hand on Sacha's shoulder, not heavily, but enough, and with the other I lightly dipped below his coat, feeling around with the tips of my fingers until I felt the rough spine of the book.

Step three: Do it quickly. It's more noticeable if you try to take something slowly—the victim has more time to notice something is happening. I swiftly pulled the journal from his coat and moved back. Grinning at my success, I pulled out the pins and unlocked the journal. Sitting on my haunches by the door, I opened the book for the second time and began to look through it. I started at the first page, my eyes skimming the words to try to find more familiar names.

Perhaps I was being optimistic, or maybe the rewards of catching Begnoche had gone to my head, but I was determined to find something else. I hadn't been lying when I had said that this could be the key to helping our king. In the past few years, there had been more and more talk about rebellion among the lower class. More talk about savages trying to kill the king. It may have been my naivety, but I had never truly believed the rumors. Now I had found evidence, and I was going to do with it what I could.

My hope, however, was slowly dwindling. I turned page after page, with not one name jumping out at me. On several pages I froze, seeing last names that seemed familiar, only to find they were slightly off, or the first names didn't match up with any of the crew.

I had almost reached the end of the book, my fingers aching and shoulders slumped. An hour or so had passed and Sacha and Orpheline had yet to do anything but grunt and twitch occasionally. The words on the pages were beginning to blur as I felt waves of exhaustion wash over me.

I turned another page slowly. My heart stopped. My eyes widened. The room grew silent and too loud all at once. My head began to throb and my fingers began to shake. I found a name I recognized. I found *two* names I recognized.

Street Informers:
Sacha Clermont
Orpheline Clermont

I was still staring at the page when a voice sounded from behind me.

"Marin, what in God's name are you doing?"

Chapter Seventeen

As I sat with the book in my hands, Sacha and Orpheline awoke. The tension in the room was palpable. Despite anything I could say to or about the siblings, they weren't stupid, and it took about a second for them to realize that I knew. That I knew that they...they were—

"Can we explain?" Orpheline asked.

I think I laughed. Maybe I didn't. Maybe I gasped at the sheer audacity of that question, and the fact that she thought she deserved a chance to explain herself. As the two of them rose to their feet, I looked at her incredulously.

"Explain?" My voice was hoarse and quiet. I sounded deadly in the silence of the room. Sacha was stony faced, angry that I had taken the journal from him but knowing that he had no place to speak up right then. "What could you possibly say that would make this better?"

"Look, I know what you want to do," she went on. "I know you want to go to Dejafosse, but I am asking you not to—"

"Don't you dare!" I hissed, my breath coming out short and sharp as I stood to face them. "Don't you dare ask me not to turn you in. I know you wouldn't do that right now. You wouldn't be so stupid, *Phe*."

"Fine," she said, her hair falling wildly in front of her eyes. "Turn us in if you must. If you think you can live with yourself, turning in the people you care about simply because a corrupt king tells you that you—"

"Wait just a second," I cut in. "*'The people I care about'*...that's what you said to me all those months ago."

Sacha looked nervously at Orpheline, his legs bent as if preparing to run, although there was nowhere for him to go. I pointed a finger at Orpheline. "You asked me what I would do for those I care about. You...you asked me that." I felt sick as I thought back on the conversation we had had about protecting friends, and the sudden shift to kindness that the two had displayed directly afterwards. I thought about how thick I was not to have seen it then. *Except you did see it,* the voice in my head said. *You just ignored it because you wanted to like them. Pathetic.*

Sacha raised his hands in a consoling manner, stepping forward. "Marin, listen—"

"NO!" I shouted, my hands trembling so hard that I squeezed them into fists, my untrimmed nails digging into my palms. "You did this on purpose, you—you lying thieves!" I held up the journal, turned to their names, and waved it at them. "You knew I might see this, might find it, so you made sure I liked you both too much to turn you in if I did find out." I was breathing heavily through my nose, feeling slightly dizzy. The two of them shuffled in front of me, Orpheline defiant while Sacha looked guiltily at his feet. I glared at the two of them, biting my lip. "Well? Aren't you going to tell me it's not true?" They didn't speak. I laughed humorlessly, blinking my eyes to stop the stinging. "Surely you two have a lie to get out of this one, too?"

Swallowing the lump in my throat, I waited for them to speak. As they remained silent, rage surged through me. I hurled the book at them, watching with satisfaction as it smacked the wall between their heads, and they both flinched violently.

"Tell me it's not true!" I shouted. They didn't move. My voice cracked. "Please."

The hold was silent. I could hear waves crashing against the sides of the ship, the once powerful rhythm now sounding like the frantic roar of some beast, trying to tear its way on board and devour the lot of us.

Orpheline sighed, her shoulders sinking. She looked me steadily in the eye through her curls.

"It's true," she said quietly.

My chin quivered suddenly and I nodded, rubbing a hand over my eyes. Maybe it was wishful thinking, but until she spoke I had clung to the hope that it might all be a lie, just another joke on silly ol' Marin, just another stupid prank of Sacha's, or payback from Orpheline for yelling at her earlier. Until she spoke, I had hoped they were who I thought they were. Just two people like myself, stuck on this ship. Just two people. Just my friends. Finding myself unable to face them any longer, I turned and stared hard at the crooked door.

"Yes, well...well, you were wrong. I don't need to go risking my life for you, a couple of criminals." I reached for the doorknob but stopped short. I couldn't bring myself to leave. Not after coming this far. I *knew* these two. Or I thought I had, at least. I spun around.

"Why?" They said nothing. "I've nearly had my back shredded twice for you now; I deserve to know that much. Why are you here? Why did you come on this ship, because you *certainly* weren't chased here by rebels, were you?"

"Why do you care?" Sacha asked, slumping against the wall, the very picture of defeat.

I folded my arms across my chest. "If nothing else, it will make me feel better."

Orpheline snorted. "You sure about that?"

"Yes." I paused. "Maybe. I'm not sure, but I have a right to know." The room was silent for a long moment before Orpheline nodded, moving to stand next to her brother, picking up the fallen book.

"Fair enough."

"Orpheline!" Sacha gaped at her, bringing a hand up to tangle his fingers in his dark hair and tug at it nervously. She shook her head.

"He's right, Sacha. He should know this." She took a deep breath. "Well, for starters, what we told you wasn't all false."

I grinned tightly and shook my head. "Of course it wasn't, just the parts about who you are and what you do."

"We really are pick-pockets, if that helps!" Sacha said, chuckling nervously. I glared at him and he sobered. "It is true that we often frequent La Chaloupe," he said, looking steadily at the floor. "It was, as you know, the meeting point in Calais for the men. The ones we told you about—the ones with the journal—they were truly there. We were there together."

"The rebels, you mean," I sneered. "The traitors."

"You watch your mouth," Orpheline said, much less afraid to look at me than her brother was. "Those are good men. Better men than any of us here. You'd be lucky to be in their company."

I clenched my fists tighter and winced as I felt one of my nails pierce my skin. "Is that what you were then? Their trusties?"

"You mock," she said, "but we were entrusted with the most important duty. It's the highest honor—the trust of good men. We didn't deserve it, either."

"How do you mean?"

Sacha eyed me warily before rubbing a hand across his tired face. "We told you, I got recognized."

I shook my head, confused. "No, you said—"

"We didn't get caught by the men at the tavern," he corrected. "We got caught by the king's men. By one of his guards." As they spoke, I slid to the floor, my back pressed tense against the door. "You said so yourself; for the past few years, it's been no secret that an uprising has been coming. The king is smart enough to realize what's going on, so he's been sending his guards to the ends of the continent in an attempt to weed out and capture anyone plotting treason."

"Good on him," I cut in bitterly. Sacha ignored me and continued.

"His guards landed in Calais about a year ago. The thing about Calais, though, is that it's too useful of a port for us to abandon it. So our top priority has been lying low and remaining unnoticed. During the day, La Chaloupe is open to anyone, but in the evening when the sun goes down, we close it to anyone not in the know. That includes the guards.

Luckily, they're too busy raiding some of the finer port taverns to care much about our little hole.

"So we were doing real well and everything, the lot of us. Phe and I arrived there only a few months ago. We'd been up in Paris living on the streets, but when a man—Levavasseur was his name—took notice of us, and what we could do, he brought us down to Calais, and we'd been there ever since, helping the men get information on what the guards did and did not know. It was going fine, until one day about a week before we ended up on this blasted ship. I was taking shift watching the guards on their daily patrol, when I see one of them has this big, fat sack of coins, dangling off his hip like an idiot. So I figure, even if Phe isn't here, a tug like that should be easy, right?"

"Your first mistake," Orpheline said, keeping her steady gaze on me.

"Right...so I get up behind this guard while he's trying to sweet talk some tavern girl, and I real quick unknot his bag and pull it from him, except what I didn't see was that it was also pinned to his hip, so when I tugged it, he felt it, and spun around yelling and shouting. I figured, 'might as well', right? I mean to say that I'd already gone so far, it would be worse not to go for it. So I pull hard once more and snap the pin, and he falls forward and I got away, if you can believe it!"

"I wouldn't call it 'getting away'," Orpheline corrected him. "You taunted the man."

"Just a bit when I was leaving."

"A bit was enough." Orpheline picked up where Sacha stopped. "It took a week for anything to come of it. The guard finally recognized Sacha."

I leaned forward, intrigued in spite of myself. "How?"

"How do you think?"

"…The bandalore?"

She nodded, and Sacha had the decency to look chastised. "The bandalore. He saw Sacha playing with it and he followed him back to La Chaloupe, bringing the rest of his men with him." She shook her head and stared at her hands. "We never saw them coming. They burst in and we just followed the older men and women and took off running. We saw the guards catch some of them. They're probably dead now. Or at least jailed. I doubt any of them got away. Sacha and I ducked out through the back and followed Levavasseur down the back alley toward the water. When we had a moment to catch our breath, he stopped us and gave us this." She shook the journal a little bit at her side. "He told us to get it to someone else in the cause. Find someone in that book and get it to them, so that they may carry on and use it."

"Why would he trust something so important with *you two*?" I asked, trying to sound as patronizing as possible.

"We're the fastest ones in Calais!" Sacha insisted, clearly affronted. He paused, embarrassed. "Or, we *were* the fastest."

"Well, Levavasseur sent us running one way while he went the other," Orpheline went on. "I think he intended for us to go to Paris. That's where most of our allies are, anyway. Except there weren't any carriages leaving for the city until that night and by then we'd be found. That's when I realized: we have men along the trail to India. There are a group of French revolutionaries in Pondicherry—scholars who are working in the colony. Sacha and I knew the ship schedules like the back of our hands, we'd been hanging around that port so long. We knew there was a ship leaving that afternoon for Pondicherry; the easiest solution was to stowaway on board and stay hidden until we reached land. Then we could wait until night and sneak ashore, and no one would ever know we were there. We just had to find a way onto the ship. Our first attempt should have worked, but we...well, we reached an impasse."

She grimaced and coughed quietly. I raised an eyebrow. "Impasse? What sort of impasse?"

Sacha snorted. "If you can even believe it, the barrel we were going to hide in was already taken." I gaped at him.

"I...you...you tried to hide in my barrel?" They both shrugged, and I leapt to my feet. "You two opened a barrel and found an unconscious boy in it, and just WALKED AWAY?"

"It's not like we realized you were asleep," Sacha said vaguely. I stared at him in wide-eyed disbelief.

"Really? You didn't realize I was—what made it unclear for you? Was it the lack of reaction to your presence or the *snoring*?" I shook my head. I had shouted a moment ago, and I couldn't let that happen again. The rest of the crew was still asleep. "Why didn't you wake me up?"

"Didn't know you were asleep," Sacha repeated.

"You thought I was just playing around in a barrel?"

"Well, you were, in actuality, weren't you? I was under the impression that the sleep was accidental."

"I could have been dead."

"Well, then, trying to wake you wouldn't have been very effective, now would it?"

"You are so—" I took a deep breath, trying to control the white-hot rage still pulsing through me, and the persistent throbbing in my temple. "Don't you realize? Had you woken me up I would have gotten out of that barrel. I would have gotten out, and you two could have gotten in, and gotten on board like that, and I wouldn't be stuck on this God-forsaken boat!" My chest was heaving, and I laughed hysterically. "That would have been the best thing for all of us."

"Maybe not, really," Sacha said pensively. "See, they found you just after we'd been found, so even if we'd hidden in the barrel, we would have been caught. At least this way we got some extra food, and our chances of getting off at India are better. I think everything that's happened was supposed to happen from the start."

I stared at him, my jaw hanging open. "That's it. I'm going to throttle him."

"Marin, calm down please."

I felt myself snap. "If either of you tells me to calm down one more time I swear to *God* I will go upstairs, get one of Begnoche's pistols, come back down and *shoot you with it.*"

The two sat motionless, staring at me, and it occurred to me that they had nothing more to say, nothing else that could sway me. I looked at them sadly. "I…I can't do this. I can't do this for you."

Sacha let out a startled breath, and jumped to his feet. "Marin, you don't understand, you *have* to!"

"Why?" I asked him, my words coming out choppy and too loud. "Why? Oh, because two lying thieves told me to? No! I won't be just another one of your homemade toys, Sacha."

"I thought we were friends," he spat through his teeth. I nodded jerkily.

"So did I. Friends don't do this to each other. They don't go this far."

"You would rather us die?"

Orpheline reached forward and grabbed her brother's sleeve. "There's no point, Sacha."

"We don't deserve to die!" Sacha said, his voice rising to a near shout. "We don't deserve to be hanged for trying to do what's right."

"I didn't deserve this," I replied, tuning to leave. I pulled the key from my neck and made quick work of the lock. As the door slipped open, Orpheline's voice stopped me for a moment.

"Should have never expected anything more. Never trust a bourgeois pig." She said nothing else. Ignoring the tear racing down my cheek, I stepped over the threshold, glancing back in time to see the faces of Orpheline and Sacha disappearing from sight. I slammed the door behind me.

Chapter Eighteen

The next day came and went in a hot blur. I had sweat pouring down my neck by noon, and the sky warned of a storm, keeping the men on their toes. "It's goin'ta hit tomorrow night. I can tell," Deole kept saying, although he seemed less worried about it than the rest of us were. Perhaps he had seen too many storms to care much about them anymore. I suppose at some point in your life, you're ready to let the storms and the sea take you.

I felt about ready to let the sea take me by the time we spotted land. My stomach had been churning all day, and with every crash of water against the sides of the *Tromperie*, my mind drifted back to the hold and the conversation with Sacha and Orpheline. I hadn't slept at all after leaving them; I had merely come up top and begun securing the rigging on the mizzenmast. As we neared the shore I felt my fingers tapping agitatedly against the ropes. I tried to ignore the sounds of the men bustling around behind me; knowing they were there did little but make me anxious. I couldn't stand the knowledge that I was again harboring a secret that put our whole country at risk. I had gone through this once with Begnoche. Why couldn't I just tell the captain? It's not like I didn't know where that would lead.

A hanging. Two hangings.

I felt a hand upon my own and looked up. Octave was standing above me, his dark brow furled in worry and the cloud-filtered light glinting on his cheek. "Are you all right, boy? You seem...out of sorts."

I nodded, swallowing dryly before attempting to smile. "I'm doing fine, thanks." I wasn't doing fine. The only two people I had felt close to for months and months turned out not only to be lying to me the whole time, but to be criminals working against the throne. I was positive things couldn't get any worse than they were.

"Is that so?" Octave asked. When I nodded again he reached past my still twitching fingers and grasped the knot I had just tied off. With one tug, the knot came loose, and I cringed as the whole bottom of the sail came undone and began floating heavily around our heads. "I ask only because this might be the worst damn rigging I ever seen."

We ducked as the sail billowed over our heads once more. He grabbed my shoulder and pulled me to the railing. Standing behind me, he steered me around until I was staring out toward the water, sea spray whipping my face.

"Breathe," he ordered. I did, feeling a slight relief as the cold, brisk air filled my lungs. "Now, speak."

I stared at the dark waters and traced the edges of the waves as they crashed together. "Are you ever so wrong about something, that...that you can't even imagine how you could have missed the truth? Have you ever tried so hard and failed so completely that you just decided that trying again wouldn't be worth it?"

He was quiet. I glanced over to see him looking down his crooked nose at me, an eyebrow raised curiously. "No, actually, can't say I have."

I felt my cheeks flush. "Well, there I have it then. Thanks for the help." I went to move but was quickly stayed by Octave's hand once more.

"You want advice, you get advice. It's not very good advice if I just tell you what you want to hear." I nodded reluctantly, and he continued. "No. I have never failed at something so thoroughly that I just gave up. That's not to say I've never failed. Believe me, you can't be alive as long as I have and not make your fair share of blunders. All that considered, nothing has ever been so bad that I just gave up and walked away."

I snorted. "Well, then you clearly haven't gone through anything as serious as what I'm facing. I mean, honestly, Octave, this could be life or death."

"Life or death, eh? Feel like sharing?"

I laughed dryly. "Not at all, actually."

He peered at me a moment longer before wiping his brow and gazing out at the horizon. His hand tightened on my shoulder. "I had a wife and a son back home, you know." My head snapped up, and I peered at him. He chuckled. "So unbelievable, is it? Mean ol' Octave can't have a family?"

"No, of course not!" I froze as he raised an eyebrow. "No, that's not what I meant—I only meant to say that of *course* you can have a family, it's just you always seemed to...well, you seem to...you hate children."

"I like you."

"Barely," I replied.

"I don't like grimy street rats sneaking aboard my ship. There is quite a big difference. Most children don't make my job as hard as you do." He chuckled once more.

I cleared my throat. "Octave?" He hummed in acknowledgement. "You said *had.* You said you had a wife and son..."

He glanced down at me. "What happened to them has happened to so many other families. There is not enough medicine in the world to help every person who needs it." His gaze stayed firm on the clouds in the distance. I, however, could not tear my eyes from his face. It was the first time on this whole journey that I truly noticed how weary he looked. The wrinkles by his eyes seemed deeper. The shadows under his eyes darker. He blinked twice and looked down at the rail. "All I'm saying, boy, is that in a place like this," he gestured to the ship, "there's no time and there's no space to give up. Things are going to happen. If you try to sail against the winds—however unfavorable they may be—you'll keel over. Let life guide you where it will, and you'll get wherever you're going a lot faster."

The silence spread over the two of us, my fingers resting against the railing. He let out a heavy breath, and I pretended to not hear how it wavered slightly. He cleared his throat. "So, want to tell me what this all important truth is that you got wrong?"

"LAND HO!" The call rang out from behind us and we turned, spotting Métivier swinging enthusiastically through the sails. Octave took one last look out at the water before taking a step away and clapping me on the shoulder.

"You're allowed on shore this time, Marin, so if I were you I'd fix that riggin' up nice and quick."

***

My first step back on land felt like flying. Or falling. Or sinking. My first step back on land felt completely bizarre. I stepped off the plank and onto the dock with the other men, expecting to feel safe and comfortable once more. Instead, I was met with the sensation of having iron in my feet. The ground felt like it was pushing back against me with every step, and I got no more than eight steps from the ship before I tripped and fell forward trying to step onto the hard wood below and underestimating how firm the earth would be. The other men laughed and hollered as I, red faced, pushed up from the ground and moved forward to join them. Deole chortled as I caught up.

"The only thing harder than adjustin' to sea legs is re-adjustin' to land legs!"

We walked with a renewed energy as we moved farther ashore. Many of the men on board had made this trip once before, some more so, and for the most part they were un-phased by the land around us. I, on the other hand, found myself open mouthed and astounded by what I saw.

This land was nothing like Paris. India was a place like none I'd never seen before. Where Paris had tall buildings and formal gardens and sparse grass cut low to the ground, Pondicherry had trees that spiraled and burst into the sky in magnificent shades of green and yellow and orange; fruits I had never seen dangled from their branches, and vines, untrimmed and unruly, twisted around their bark. High above us birds sang foreign tunes from foreign bills, and in the dirt were the footprints of creatures I had never dreamed of. As we passed houses and markets, I felt an overwhelming sense of homesickness sweep over me.

Whether the sensation was for Paris or the *Tromperie* I could not decide.

That night was devoted to merriment. The men were delighted to be off the ship, and even more so to be in the company of foreign women. We sat under a small canopy near the jungle's edge, and we whiled away the evening in pleasant company as the sun began to sink. The men sang songs to impress the natives—who seemed entirely bemused and uninterested—and drank as much as they were given. I myself was passed a flask of some strong smelling drink, but after several sips I coughed myself into a fit and passed the flask to the next man over.

The energy was infectious, and I smiled to think that this was how the men spent every landing. Had they done this in Africa as well? Sat among the people there and grinned and taken in everything so casually? To see so much of the world that it no longer catches your eye must be a great achievement, I thought to myself. Yet I could not imagine ever wanting to be un-moved by places like this. Such beauty should never grow so common as to be unappreciated.

The night was so dazzling that I nearly forgot about Sacha and Orpheline and the secrets left behind on the Tromperie. It was not until Dejafosse joined us in our festivities that the full gravitas of the situation hit. He began to joke with the men that the noose was prepared, that the hanging would be in the morning, that Begnoche wouldn't seem so grand dangling from a tree. The air began to feel too warm, and I longed to tell our hosts to put out the fire. Despite the darkness of the sky, I felt as though a blinding light was shining on me, harsh and unforgiving. It was still early evening, and I knew that most of the men would not be sleeping tonight, yet my body was already heavy with exhaustion.

I looked around me at the other sailors. I saw Gérard, away from the crow's nest for possibly the first time since we set sail; I saw Métivier spilling ale on himself as he talked to a pretty local girl. Deole, sitting with some of the younger men, was telling a story he had no doubt told a thousand times, while all of the men listened with rapt fascination; toward the back of the space, Octave and Dejafosse sat with their heads close together, talking other about some matter or another.

Good men. These were good men. If I knew one thing with certainty it was that these men were of the best stock. They had done nothing but good for me, given the circumstances, and they deserved nothing but respect in return. My whole family was waiting at home declaring allegiance to the king—my family! My mother, father, brother—the best people anyone could know.

These were kind, intelligent, *good* people. They all believed in our country. I would not let two rogue children stop me from standing along side these good people, no matter how...fond of them I may have become.

Before I was fully aware of it, I was weaving through the men toward Octave and Dejafosse. I reached them as Dejafosse took a swig of ale, his head thrown back in mirth. Both men looked at me curiously as I came to a halt. Octave grinned, though in his eyes I could see a question. Dejafosse, on the other hand, let out a bark of laughter and beckoned me with one large hand, the other trying to balance his pint while stroking his beard.

"Ah! Marin, my boy! Come sit with us and tell us a story of high society."

I inhaled deeply. "No, sir, I actually have something else to tell you."

He chortled again. "I'm sure you do! Tell me all about that fine home'a yours. Lots of pretty girls, eh?"

"Fine, yes, lots of girls—look, captain," I tried once more. Octave was quietly watching me, a drink in his hand and a wary glint in his eye. "It's about the...the rebellion."

The captain's red face twisted in what I could only assume was supposed to be a look of the utmost seriousness. Behind us the men began singing some low-pitched love song that made the women giggle and roll their eyes. The song cut into our quiet conversation, and I raised my voice to ensure the captain would hear me.

"It's just that—although I know we found Begnoche—"

"*I'll sail these seven seas and seven thousand more—*"

"We found Begnoche? No, no! My boy, *you* found Begnoche! Good thing, too! Can't have scum like him aboard."

"Very true, sir. However, I've found recently—quite recently, actually—that there is more to this plot than just Begnoche—"

"*For the lovely young lady of all of my dreams—*"

"—And I need to tell you what I've learned so that you may go forward from here regarding the matter."

"*Came poundin' and scratchin' and lettin' out screams—*"

I took a deep breath and braced myself. "It is about the two stowaways you've got in the hold. I have come across proof—strong proof—that...that they too are..."

"*And throwin' her petticoats and rippin' the seams—*"

Dejafosse rolled his eyes and took another sip of ale. "Spit it out, boy."

"*At my best mate Finnegan's cabin door!*"

"They are also members of the rebellion, working with Begnoche and many other men and women."

"Oy, what was that?" One of the men shouted in our direction. They had finished singing behind me and were now looking over at the three of us curiously. I felt small beneath their gaze.

"You mind your own business, then," Dejafosse called back. His face was now pensive as he took in my anxious stance. He stroked his thick beard in thought, while next to him Octave was giving me a look that was not nearly as surprised as I would have liked it to be.

Finally, Dejafosse spoke again. He said, "You're sure about this then?"

"Why would I lie to you now?"

"You got quite a nice reward when you turned in Begnoche," he said easily, sipping lightly from his pint. "Perhaps you want the same treatment again."

I shook my head. "No. I wouldn't...I don't want to say this but I know I must. Those two are no different than Begnoche. Younger perhaps, but just as wicked in intent. I have proof that they are who I say they are."

Octave was frowning at me, his lips curled in in distaste. "Marin, wait just a moment…"

"No, Octave, it's fine." I could feel my resolve cracking already, and I was certain that nothing Octave had to say would make this easier on me. "Captain, your word?"

He seemed to think about it for a moment before nodding heavily, his chin nearly hitting his chest. "All right, then, Marin m'boy. If you say it, I believe it. You've got a good history in weedin' out rats!" He nudged Octave with his elbow and laughed loudly, his grin making his eyes squint. "Eh, Octave? Boy's got a pretty good history?"

Octave nodded slowly, still eyeing me reproachfully. "Aye, sir. He's a good man. Always looking out for his own. Right, Marin?"

"Right," I replied, though I found myself staring down at the dirt and my ripped boots rather than at him.

Dejafosse belched loudly and pounded one meaty fist on his knee. "All right, then, that's all settled! We're finishing Begnoche off tomorrow. The man wanted it done at night. He said he didn't want to be sweatin' when he hanged, but I think he just don't want anyone lookin' at his sorry face." He laughed loudly again and I shivered, chills running along my limbs. Octave had stopped drinking completely. "So we'll get him done with during the day naturally. I'll have the other men draw up two more ropes, and we'll have the rats done in tomorrow night, at sun fall."

I nodded sharply, swallowing the swell of emotion that was threatening to choke me. With one last pat on my shoulder, Dejafosse bid me good night, and I pivoted on one heel and rushed from the canopy. Once my feet hit the edge of the shaded space I found I couldn't stop them. I found I didn't want to. So instead I found the tracks from the carriages in the dirt and began to follow those, and I followed them until they too ended and then I found the footsteps of our crew and I began to follow those. I walked through the jungle path as swiftly as I could, stubbornly refusing to acknowledge the tears that fell from my eyes. I ignored them until it began to rain, at which point the raindrops fell cold on my face and it became impossible to discern my emotions from the weather. By the time I reached the *Tromperie* the ground had turned muddy and thick, and I trudged up the planks of the dock and onto the silent ship.

I made my way to the starboard bow of the ship and stepped around the foremast, moving onto the bowsprit. I began to walk forward on it. I thought back to when I was only ten years of age, and some street urchins had taken to performing outside my house. A woman had walked on a rope she tied between two windows over an alley, and she walked it gracefully, her arms stretched out like she was flying. I was so scared she would fall. Now I spread my arms out, too, and with my eyes shut against the rain, I began to walk across the bowsprit. I felt myself waver, and my heart skipped. My blind confidence failing me, I lowered myself to the wooden beam and sat down, my legs hanging over the side.

"Marin!" I turned as Octave's voice echoed across the ship. I squinted to see him through the rain.

"Ahoy there, Octave! Care to join me?" I tried to laugh, but it came out sounding strangled and fake.

"Care to get the hell off my ship?" he shouted back, his hands cupped around his mouth. In no mood to argue I stood back up, but as I took my first step toward him, my right foot slipped on the wet wood and I slid, falling through the air quickly. Reflexively I lunged out, wrapping my left leg around the beam and grabbing onto it with both hands. I ended up dangling from the bottom of the beam, only a bit above the deck. "Jesus, boy, you're going to get yourself killed!"

Below me the water crashed and roared against the sides of the ship. We had docked in shallow enough water that were I to fall at this moment, my body would surely crash against the ocean floor. I felt hands gripping my upper arms, and I let go of the beam, flailing slightly before finding purchase on Octave's shoulders. "Get back up here, you lousy brat," he was grunting, pulling me until one of my knees was resting against the bowsprit. He let go of my arm with one hand, only to wrap it around my waist and swing me away from the open air, dropping me onto the deck with little kindness. I looked over his shoulder to the water I'd been hanging above moments before and whistled low.

"That could've gone much worse, all things considered." His hand smacked me across the back of my head. "What earth was that for?" I spluttered, clutching my skull.

"Are you completely daft? You were two seconds from drowning! What were you thinking, going out there in this weather?" He was breathing heavily through flared nostrils.

"I wasn't thinking anything, I...I was bored," I lied.

"Bored?" he asked incredulously. "You were bored? Of course! Yes, Marin can risk life and limb because he's *bored*! God forbid no one comes along and saves him this time."

"But you did come along."

He opened his mouth to speak, but instead just exhaled heavily, moving to sit across from me on the wet planks. We sat in numb silence and listened to wind howling in the sails. My clothes had soaked through to the bone and my hair, at this point long and untamed, was matted to my cheeks. I sniffed loudly and looked Octave in the eyes.

"I don't want them to die."

He smiled grimly, running his hand over his face. "I know you don't, Marin."

"They deserve to, though, don't they?" I asked.

"Some would say so, yes."

"Would you say so?"

He shrugged his heavy shoulders, turning his face skyward and letting the rain hit it. I sniffed again and swiped at my eyes. "They should die, though, just like Begnoche. I turned Begnoche in and...and I celebrated. He's going to be hanged tomorrow, and I'm glad! I should be celebrating the death of Orph—of the traitors, too." I stumbled over their names and bit my tongue.

"You weren't friends with Begnoche," Octave told me gently, his blue eyes dim in the dark light.

I scoffed, curling in on myself and wrapping my hands around my ankles. "I'm not friends with these two, either."

He raised an eyebrow. "Marin." I groaned, hitting my head against my knees once and letting it rest there.

"Fine. I am their friend. I am the friend of two low-life, treasonous pick-pockets. What does that make me?" I lifted my head up and stared at him, part of me hoping he'd have the answer, part of me not wanting to know what that answer was. "Dear God, my father will skin me when I return home!"

"He won't do," Octave said. "You've not done anything wrong. You turned in everyone you're obligated to turn in. It should all be smooth sailing from here on out, except…"

He trailed off, and I swallowed hard. "Except I don't want them to die," I repeated. He nodded. Digging my nails into my shins I gritted my teeth and shook my head, wishing I could get Sacha and Orpheline's faces from my mind. "They're just as bad as Begnoche, though!" I protested, more to myself than to Octave. "How I feel about them should make no difference."

He sighed heavily, and I had a sudden wish never to hear another sigh again. There were too many of them. He stood, water dripping from his frame, and held out a hand for me to take. I took it and stood, feeling heavy with the water soaking through me. He pushed the wet bangs from my forehead, then rested his hands on my shoulders and spoke softly.

"The way you feel about them makes *all* the difference in the world. We are human beings, Marin; we're not meant to look at the world in facts and absolutes. Life is circumstantial. Whether Marie and Louis are going to die or not is up to the king. Whether or not they truly deserve to die is up to the people who know them." I chuckled weakly, and he frowned. "What?"

"You never learned their real names, did you?"

He thought for a moment before shaking his head. "No, I don't suppose I did."

"Clermont," I told him. "Their names are Orpheline and Sacha Clermont. And they are good people."

He smiled sadly at me and clapped me on the shoulder. "I'm certain they are, Marin. I'm certain they are."

Chapter Nineteen

Begnoche was being hanged in five minutes. Sacha and Orpheline were being hanged that night. The men and I were all gathered at a post near the center of the town, our coats pulled tight around us against the cold. The storm that had begun the day before hadn't subsided in the least over the course of the night. If anything it had gained momentum, the winds raging around us and forcing the men to dig their heels into the dirt in order to avoid being blown over. We were all chilled and shivering, and I couldn't stop sneezing. After my conversation with Octave the previous night, I never fully dried and felt cold to my core.

I could barely see Begnoche and Dejafosse through the rain, yet I was able to make out the noose swinging back and forth. Octave stood at the base of the platform's stairs and was looking morbidly at the ground. Next to me was Métivier, trembling in either excitement or fear. He kept nudging me with his elbow.

"Never seen a hangin' before, I haven't. Heard of a lot of 'em though! Supposed to be somethin', eh?" He was bouncing on the balls of his feet, and I felt nauseous. I hadn't eaten since breakfast the past day and hadn't slept that night and was too full of nerves to speak. Most of the sailors had come ashore to see this. Deole outright refused to attend the hanging, saying he had seen enough deaths for a lifetime. I wished I could've said the same thing, but unfortunately the men were adamant that the person who caught Begnoche in the first place should be present for his execution.

Dejafosse climbed onto the platform, guiding Begnoche along with him. Together they ascended the stairs and walked to the middle of the platform. A native man I didn't know or care to know stepped forward and placed the noose around Begnoche's neck before tightening it. Dejafosse stepped forward and addressed the men.

"For crimes committed against His Majesty, King Louis of France, this man shall now be hanged by the neck until dead!" He sounded distorted through the winds. I felt Métivier nudge me again, and I snapped at him.

"What *is* it?"

"Octave wanted me to get the key to the gun room from you. He's goin' to do inventory today."

"Why can't I do it?"

He shrugged, eyes fixed on Begnoche. "Said somethin' about you bein' too tired to swab a deck, let alone manage guns."

I snorted lightly and pulled the cord from my neck, taking the key to the gunroom and giving it to Métivier, keeping the key to the hold in its place. I put the cord back on my neck.

"Much obliged." He didn't say another word, too interested in the activity on the platform to pay me any mind. Dejafosse was making a speech about loyalty to king and country, and next to me the men were all shaking, and I was shaking though I no longer felt cold. I watched as the native man stepped forward to draw a black sack over Begnoche's head. I wondered if it was for him or for us. That's when it became too much for me. Without a face there to assure me that it was Begnoche, I now saw Sacha standing on the platform.

His eyes were dark, and he was glaring, copying Dejafosse in a wicked voice. *For king and for country, Marin? That's all there is to you, king and country.* I shook my head and looked up again only to see Orpheline staring back at me, except her eyes were not her eyes—they were eyes clouded over and white with death. Her skin was wet and pale, and she too was shouting to me across the heads of the sailors, her voice high pitched and wicked. *Going to just stand there then? Watch us die then sail home to mother? I swear, you're even more pathetic than I thought.* I felt anger coursing through me—fury that I was seeing an Orpheline and a Sacha who were not *really* Sacha and Orpheline at all. They were some foul mockeries, polluted by the revolution, as all good things are. I clenched my eyes tight and rubbed my temple. My head was beginning to throb, and I wished for nothing more than a tonic to soothe the ache inside me. I remembered Orpheline's cough. I remembered getting the tonic for her. I remembered the way she looked at me afterwards. *Thank you, Marin.* I remembered Sacha sticking his neck out for me, when he didn't have to. *Consider it returning a favor.*

On the platform, Dejafosse had stopped speaking. He took a step back, and my heart leapt into my throat, and I *knew* what was about to happen and didn't want to see it. I didn't want to see this man die in front of me. I didn't want to see him die and…and I didn't want to see my friends die, either. I couldn't let them die. I had told them I wouldn't let them get hurt on this trip. *You promised, remember?*

Dejafosse had his hand on a lever when he spoke. "May the Lord have mercy on his soul."

He pulled the lever. The floor beneath Begnoche's feet fell away, and before I could see the rope pull taught, I had already spun around and was pushing through the men. Shoving them out of my way as quickly as I could, I ignored the shouts and calls of my name as I went. I thought perhaps I heard Octave calling for me as I ran but spared no thought to him, refusing to stop and look around for fear that I might not start moving again. And I had to keep moving. I had to get back to the ship.

I could barely see as I fled, the rain whipping against my face and making my cheeks sting, but I had run this path more than five times now and memory guided me back to the ship. Every few seconds I glanced behind me, certain I could still hear the yells of the men. By now, Dejafosse most definitely would have noticed my absence, and even if he hadn't, I doubted that Octave would let me flee without following. Not after last night's incident.

I tripped and fell as I reached the edge of the tree line, the front of my body stained with mud and sand. Pushing myself up I ran toward the shore, letting out a whoop when I saw the *Tromperie* ahead, bobbing innocently on the waves. I cursed as I saw Gérard sitting watch at the end of the dock, clearly making sure nobody came on board the ship unmonitored.

Realizing I wouldn't be able to sneak by Gérard unseen, I thought quickly. I shed my jacket—it was too heavy to swim with in these conditions—and dove head first into the crushing waters on the other side of the ship from the dock.

I felt my ears pop as I became immersed in the ocean, the frigid cold of the water numbing my fingers in an instant. I kept my eyes open long enough to spot the mass of the ship to my right, and then I closed them and swam in the direction of it, kicking my legs out wildly.

I was so overjoyed to finally feel the planks against my fingers that I let out a triumphant shout, closing my mouth quickly as I felt freezing water filling it. Moving up the side of the ship, I burst through the water's surface and gasped in air, looking around me for the anchor chain. I spotted it a ways down the ship, toward the stern, and began to move toward it, keeping my palms pressed against the ship. I reached it swiftly and wrapped my hands around it—thankful for the callouses I had formed in the past months—and began to pull myself up the length of it.

I had seen more than one of the older men climbing the rigging like this during our journey, and while they made it seem as easy as walking up the stairs, I found myself struggling to breathe as I snaked my way up the chain, my feet sliding against the wood as I tried to use them to walk up the ship's side. Soon enough my arms and legs began to burn, and callouses alone were doing nothing to stop the pain in my hands. I feared I might not make it to the deck, but thought once more of my purpose and continued to climb. My chest was aching and it took me far more time than seemed reasonable to reach the rail. As I swung one sore leg over the bannister and placed it on the deck, I heard a voice through the rain and looked toward the entrance to below decks.

"What are yuh doin', Marin? You shouldn' be out in this sort'a weather!" Deole stood within the open door, his dark hands clutching a woolen blanket around his shoulders. I ran across the deck to where he stood, sliding to a halt in front of him and placing my hands on the doorframe for balance.

"Deole! I need your help." I knew the other men would be on their way back to the ship now—Octave and Dejafosse at least—to see where I had gone so quickly. The captain would probably think the hanging made me sick or something, but Octave would know better. He would know what I was here to do. Deole was looking at me apprehensively.

"What can I do for you, Marin?" he asked. I glanced over the edge of the ship to the shore, where I could not yet see anyone coming through the trees to the ship. I looked back to Deole.

"The captain may be coming here very soon. If he does, say nothing about seeing me. I wasn't here."

He looked worried now. "An' where should I tell him that you are?"

"Nowhere," I told him quickly, hoping he understood. "Don't lie to him, don't do that for me. Just...tell him you haven't seen me." I made to move past him but stopped when his thin fingers wrapped around my wrist. He spoke from behind me.

"Marin...boy, what are you doin' here?"

I shook my head, staring down the stairs in front of me, lit by several candlesticks on the walls. "Nothing good." I turned my head to smile at him over my shoulder. "Thank you for all of your help, Deole."

He smiled gently at me, shrugging one shoulder. The wrinkles by his eyes deepened and he let go of me slowly. "All I did was lock yuh in a closet," he said, and I laughed.

"Aye, and thank God for that." I nodded goodbye and turned, dashing down the stairs to the hold. I careened down the halls, past the galley and the capstan and the orlop and the sick bay until I turned the final corner, tripping as I stepped in front of the door behind which I'd spent the last few months. I reached up to my neck and pulled the key from it. Shoving it into the lock, I made to turn it, frowning when it would not give.

"What in the world..." I muttered, pulling the key up to my face and examining it closely. My eye caught sight of the small dent in the key's ring and I cursed; I had given Métivier the key to the hold, and the key that I now held went to the gunroom. "You're kidding me." I spun around, glancing nervously around the corner. It was only a matter of time before Dejafosse came barreling down the stairs and throttled me. Octave would tell him what I was doing, he would have to. Loyal to a fault, Octave. Groaning quietly, I ran a hand through my wet hair anxiously, freezing when I felt the cool brush of metal on my fingers.

The pins.

I reached up and sifted through my locks, extracting Deole's pins and laughing triumphantly as I knelt down and pushed them into the keyhole. After a moment of twisting and pressing, I heard the soft click and the door swung open.

For a moment I felt as though this was my first day on the ship, and a wave of déja vu swept over me as I took in the siblings. They were pressed together against the back wall of the hold, hunched over with their heads down and their hands intertwined. As I stood in the doorway, Orpheline looked up, and I watched with vague satisfaction as her eyes widened a fraction. She nudged her sleeping brother in his ribs, waking him. He blearily rubbed his eyes.

"Whus goin' on?" he asked and peered up at me through his curled bangs. "What d'you want?"

I looked at him, keeping my face blank. "Begnoche is dead."

They blanched a bit, and Orpheline scowled darkly at me. "Come down here just to throw it in our faces, have you? Come to lecture us on right and wrong?"

"I could do that," I agreed. "Though, I'm not sure we have the time for a lecture if we want to get off this ship before the crew catches us."

A moment passed. Then, with a groan, Orpheline dropped her head into her hands.

"You're terrible," she muttered, though the smile on her face gave her away. "I thought you were going to let us get hanged." Sacha shot up to his knees and gaped at me, his eyes lighting up and an excited smile crossing his face.

"You rogue!" he cried joyfully. "You knave! You ruddy *scoundrel*—you do know you're helping two no good criminals, don't you?"

I shrugged, lowering my hands to my hips. "Maybe not *no* good." I turned and checked the hall, releasing a breath of relief when I saw nobody approaching. I looked back at the siblings. "We need to go, now. We've not got much time."

The two nodded, and I stepped forward, offering them each a hand and pulling them up. Sacha grabbed the journal from the floor and thrust it into his coat. Orpheline brushed off the seat of her nightgown. I made to leave.

"Marin," she called, and I stopped, looking at her.

"What is it?"

She wrung her hands nervously. "You sure about this?" I opened my mouth to speak but she hurried on. "You're not going to come back from something like this. This...this is *treason*, Marin."

"She's right," Sacha piped in. "What changed your mind?"

I looked at the two of them, standing there in their mismatched clothes and the last few months came flooding back to me. Eating stolen food, discussing stolen books, risking life and limb for each other...I thought back on all of this.

"I'm not doing this because I agree with your morals," I told them. "I think you're wrong, and I think you're going to lose this war...but I saw what they did to Begnoche. It was hard enough seeing that happen, and I wasn't even fond of the man. I just...I couldn't let you die." I shrugged one shoulder dismissively. "Just consider it...returning a favor." I turned and dashed out of the hold and with a laugh, Sacha—pulling Orpheline by her hand—came running out after me.

Chapter Twenty

We made it down the hall at a record speed, and as we turned the corner that led to the decks Orpheline grabbed me suddenly. "Marin, stop. *Listen,*" she whispered. I did and groaned quietly. I could hear the voices of the men coming from the top of the stairs. I looked at the two of them and gestured to the voices.

"Well?"

They looked at me blankly. Sacha said, "What do you want us to do?"

"You're the criminals!" I said. "What do you suggest?"

Sacha growled, frustrated, and closed his eyes for a second. "We sneak by them. Light on our feet. Easy."

"Can we do that?" I asked uncertainly.

He nodded and grinned nervously, rubbing his neck. "Sure, course we can. I'll just check how many there are. Stay here." He moved past Orpheline and I and went around the corner. Ten seconds later he reappeared, eyes wide. "Scratch that—terrible idea."

Orpheline whacked the back of his head lightly. "How many men are out there?"

"Don't know. How many men are on this ship, Marin?"

"About one hundred."

"Interesting. I'd say there's about one hundred men out there."

I cursed, kicking the wall. "Fantastic. That's just brilliant. Now what do we do?"

"You could always go distract them, and we could make a run for it!" Sacha suggested, patting me on the back. I raised an eyebrow at him.

"I could always go stick you back in the hold and do a jig at your hanging."

Orpheline smacked both of us this time. "Would you two keep quiet? You're going to get us all caught." She crossed her arms and bit her lip, her face taking on a pensive expression. After a minute, her eyes lit up. "Got it. There's the flood stairs, aren't there—on the other side of the ship toward the stern? We can go take those."

I looked at her in astonishment. "How did you know about those?"

"Most ships have them, Marin," she said, peering around the corner once more. She looked back at me. "Honestly, I'm a little disappointed you didn't think of those immediately. Let's go." She grabbed her brother and me by our sleeves and began to tug. We ran through the dank halls, trying to avoid any loud thumping as our feet hit the floor. I could hear the pounding of the rain on the outside of the ship and drops of water were falling through the cracks in the ceiling and dripping down my already drenched neck.

The flood stairs were on the farthest end of the ship from the hold, and in order to get to them we'd first have to scale a smaller, twisted set of stairs that led us past the men's sleeping quarters and the gunroom. The three of us reached the end of the hall, and Sacha climbed the first step, then froze.

"Damn," he muttered and turned to look at us, anger and disappointment clear on his face. "Listen—there's someone up there, too."

Orpheline and I huffed, and she ran a hand through her hair. Moving around Sacha, I began to ascend the stairs, one at a time. Behind me, Orpheline was whispering urgently. "Sacha, you said most of the men are top deck, right?"

"Certainly seemed like it, yes."

"In that case there can't be too many people at the top of these stairs," she said. I understood her point, yet I felt the need to warn her that many of the sailors aboard this ship were more than strong enough to tear apart three children. I reached the top of the stairs, the sounds of light whistling coming from the hall. I took a deep breath and peered around the corner. What I saw made me laugh quietly in delight. I hurried back down the few steps and gave the two a smile.

"No need to fear—It's just one man, and we can take him."

Sacha seemed unconvinced. "How can you be sure?"

"It's Métivier," I drawled, breathing easy. "Trust me, we can handle Métivier." They both nodded, and I beckoned them to follow me. We crept up the stairs once more, and casually I turned the corner, putting out a hand to stop them from following.

"Hello, Métivier!" I said pleasantly. Startled, he jumped up from where he had been leaning against the wall. His eyes widened, and he glanced over his shoulder nervously.

"Marin! Hello there, mate...where'd you run off to?" He was stuttering slightly, and I frowned.

"What, you mean at the hanging? Oh, well, I remembered I'd tied one of the riggings off incorrectly this morning if you can believe it, so I came back to fix it."

"You ran away quickly. Seemed scared, you did."

"I didn't want us losing a sail, did I?"

He nodded absently. "You weren't top deck when we came back a few minutes ago." He looked over his shoulder again.

I thought quickly. "I finished the rigging so I came down to get some rest. Didn't sleep well in this storm last night."

"I see," he said. He looked behind him a third time and coughed.

"You expecting somebody, Métivier?" I asked.

He blinked wide-eyed and put his hands out, as if trying to soothe me. "Well, to be honest there, Marin, the captain said to let him know if we saw you."

"Why would he want that?"

"Well, he seemed to be worried you were doing somethin'...not good," he mumbled. "And I'm a tad inclined to believe him, seein' as you're now lyin' to me."

My palms began to itch with nerves, and I smiled at Métivier, trying to seem as innocent as possible. "Lying? Why would you say that?"

"It's just that you said that you came down to get some rest, but I've been here for quite a while now, and haven't seen you. So I know you wasn't in the men's quarters."

"I see," I said, feeling my confidence failing and wishing I were as good at lying as Sacha. "Right well…I stopped by the hold to give food to the prisoners first. That's all."

He didn't seem convinced. "So why didn' you just tell me that?"

I went to respond, but at that moment a shout came from behind him, and we both looked at the stairs that led to the deck.

"Métivier! Keep an eye out for L'Émule! The two stowaways aren't in the hold!"

With wild eyes Métivier spun around and pointed at me, his finger shaking. "Y-you let them out, didn' you?"

The shout came again. "Did you hear me, boy? The stowaways have escaped!"

"You let them out!" Métivier repeated, laughing a little hysterically, clearly realizing he had the opportunity to be helpful for the first time since stepping aboard the ship. He began to holler back up the stairs. "I got 'im! Oy, you hear me? MARIN'S HERE!"

I groaned in frustration. "We haven't got time for this," I hissed, before turning around. "Sacha—"

"Way ahead of you," Sacha said, jumping out from behind the corner and running at Métivier—who was still facing away from us—and bowling him over. He turned the older boy onto his back and, without sparing a moment for his shocked cry, pulled him up by the collar and hit him square in the cheek. Métivier's head hit the ground with a thud, and Sacha stood. Orpheline appeared next to me and sighed.

"You needn't have hit him quite so hard."

"He was annoying me," Sacha said dismissively. He looked at me and nodded for me to speak. "What next, Captain?"

I laughed and pointed toward the stairs. "Up those stairs and over the rails. Then we're on land and free."

Perhaps we might have made it. Perhaps there was some way in which we could have gotten up unnoticed and off the ship without any trouble. However, we never got to find out, for at that moment the last person in the world I wanted to see called out from the stairs.

"Hold the boy there, I'm coming down." It was Dejafosse. Sacha, Orpheline, and I stared at one another in terror. Orpheline shook me.

"Think, Marin. *Think.*"

Shaking my head, I looked helplessly at her. That's when I felt it—bouncing against my chest as I shook my head—the key to the gunroom. I grabbed their fingers and pulled them back down the hall several steps. We skidded to a halt in front of the door, and I ripped the key from my neck, unlocking the door as quick as I could, the cool metal slippery in my sweaty grasp. I swung the door open and was shoved inside by the siblings. I closed the door just as the sound of footsteps reached our ears. The room was dark, the only light coming from the cracks around the door and the light dripping in from the ceiling. Sacha nudged me.

"What are we doing?" he mouthed at me.

"Hiding," I mouthed back. He frowned and leaned in.

"Why aren't we shooting?"

Orpheline reached over and flicked his ear. "You want to shoot so badly, pick a gun and go, but we aren't in a position for you to be complaining."

"Oh, Marin..." We froze as Dejafosse's voice floated through the door. "Where'd you go, Marin? I have to say I'm disappointed. When Octave told me you might've taken the rats from their cage I was shocked, but now? I'm not surprised, really. You were a pain in my side from the moment you came aboard my ship."

I felt someone brush up against me and turned to find Sacha reaching over our heads to one of the guns mounted on the wall. His sister and I stared at him as he took down a flintlock pistol and several pellets from a leather sack. We stood, frozen, as he loaded the pistol and cocked it against his side. He caught my wide eyes and gave me a resigned nod.

"There's no way around it," he whispered.

Orpheline looked at me questioningly. "Marin? Do we have any other options?"

I took a deep breath and clenched my eyes shut, wishing for the thousandth time since coming aboard that I were simply at home in my warm bed, about to wake up from a terrible dream. I shook my head. "No. We have no other way out. He has a gun; this just levels our chances."

She nodded at her brother, who seemed pale in the darkness. "On three then." I nodded in return.

"One."

"Two."

"...Three!" I slammed the door open and ran out, the two of them behind me. Dejafosse stood at the foot of the stairs, his round face red with anger and his chest heaving. He smirked at the three of us, his own gun tapping lightly against his thigh. Sacha pointed the pistol at him.

"Hello, you three. Why don't we all settle down and talk about this like adults?"

I laughed humorlessly. "Settle down? Why, so that you can keep us here until they have three nooses ready for us? No thank you, *sir.*"

"Hang you? Marin, I wouldn't dream of it. I just want to make sure you get home safely to your father and mother. Just give up the traitors and come with me, and we can make sure you get home safe and sound. You want that, too, don't you, son?" I tensed, and I knew Orpheline felt it. She looked at me, and I looked at her, and I thought *yes,* I *do* want to be home with my parents. I wanted to be at home with a good meal that consisted of more than dry bread and dry meat; I wanted to be sitting in front of a fire, wearing clothes other than the same shirt and pants and jacket that I'd been wearing for four months, talking with my family. I wanted to be safe and know that nothing could touch me. I wanted that.

But more than that, I wanted these two to be okay. Nothing would pry me from their sides. I winked at Orpheline and looked back to Dejafosse. "I've made my choice, Dejafosse. I'm not easily bought."

The smile melted from his face, and he sneered at us. "You want to get off this ship? You'll have to get past me first, boy."

"If you insist," I said. I covered my ears and shouted, "Sacha, SHOOT!"

Nothing happened. I pulled my fingers from my ears and looked at Sacha. He hadn't moved; he was shaking like a leaf, his eyes wide as saucers and the gun still aimed at the captain. I gaped at him. "Sacha, why aren't you shooting?"

"I've never shot anyone!" he snapped, before pushing the gun into my hands. "Here, you do it."

Dejafosse began to roar with laughter. "I'd pick my side more carefully next time, Marin!" he wheezed.

I stared at the weapon. "What do you expect me to do?"

"Shoot!" Orpheline cried. "If you're going to shoot him just do it! Oh for the love of—*give me the damn thing*!" She wrenched the pistol from my hand and, without a moment's hesitation, fired the gun at the still laughing Dejafosse. I looked on in shock as he screamed, grabbing his now bleeding leg and falling to the floor.

"You worthless brat!" he was screeching at Orpheline, the color draining from his face. His gun had tumbled from his hands as he fell and he grabbed for it weakly, before shouting in pain and grabbing his leg again. Sacha was staring at his sister in amazement.

"Phe, you just shot a man."

She rolled her eyes at him. "Nice of you to notice. Now, if you'd be so kind, Marin, I think now is a good time for us to get the hell off this ruddy boat."

I shook myself out of my shocked reverie and nodded, walking slowly toward Dejafosse and, behind him, the stairs. As I reached him I glanced down and grimaced. He was glaring up at me, looking murderous and close to fainting at the same time. He made a pathetic grab for me, but couldn't get a firm hold of my arm. I gently tugged my sleeve from his grip, stepping over him and onto the stairs. I heard Orpheline and Sacha following me, and a sudden yelp of pain from the captain gave me the impression that one of them had stepped on him. We reached the trapdoor to the top deck and with one last reassuring look to the both of them, I pushed it upward and stepped into the open air.

At first glance the top deck seemed fine. Orpheline and Sacha followed me out and we blinked at the rain. It was falling gently now, and the air seemed thick and moist in the Indian heat. Sacha nudged me and grinned.

"That wasn't so difficult, was it?" He laughed as his sister giggled quietly. "It's all easy from here, aye?"

"I wouldn't be so sure about that, young ones."

We turned around and froze. The rest of the deck was covered with men, all gazing at us. Octave stood at the front, looking sadly at me. Orpheline raised the gun at him now, and I gulped. "Octave! Imagine the chances of running into you here."

"You didn't really think nobody would hear a gunshot, did you?" he asked. I shrugged and smiled nervously, my chest tightening as we looked at each other. He shook his head and sighed. "Is this it then?" he asked me quietly, his voice heavy with sorrow. "You've chosen, then?"

I stared back at him sadly and tried to find a way to explain this all to him. However, deep down I knew that, no matter how unhappy he was about it, he already understood. He didn't need it to be explained to him. "This isn't me not choosing you," I told him. "This isn't me not choosing our king or our country. This is just..." I waved my hands in a search for the words. "This is just me choosing them, too."

We were speaking too quietly for the men to hear us well, and I saw them craning their necks behind him. Octave looked searchingly at me for a moment more, then glanced at Sacha and Orpheline. Then he raised his hands above his head and took a step back.

"The girl has a gun," he called over his shoulder, the men tensing immediately. "She's already shot our captain, and she's willing to shoot again. Everybody stay where you stand." He lowered his voice again. "Go. Go now, and I better not see you again on this ship."

That was enough for the siblings, who turned to run again, Orpheline grabbing my hand as we went. Octave called out to me once more. "Marin, you understand me?" I turned back around and looked at the man, my brown eyes meeting his tired blue ones. He looked at me purposefully. "*I better not find you aboard this ship again*, aye?" I nodded slowly, and his mouth twitched upwards for a moment. "Go," he said.

We ran.

I could see the tops of the ladder propped against the port side of the ship and we dashed toward it. The three of us quickly exchanged nods and scrambled down it, Orpheline in front, Sacha second, and me scurrying down last. We dropped the last few feet onto the dock. Orpheline grabbed for me once more and with a final look at the *Tromperie*, we took off running to the jungle.

We didn't take the jungle path, for that was too easily followed. Instead, we found a clearing in the trees and pushed through it, running blindly. We ran until our sides hurt, until our breaths came sharp and painful and our bodies were dripping sweat and our feet ached. We kept running. We didn't stop until the rain stopped, and by that point we'd been fleeing for almost an hour, pausing only occasionally to lean silently against trees for a few moments while we caught our breath. We couldn't risk staying in one place for too long, for fear that we'd be caught.

Once we finally ceased our mad running, we tumbled to the ground and lay on our backs with our chests heaving. For minutes we said nothing, just letting our breathing even out. After a while I assumed the other two had fallen asleep and began to drift off myself, only to be brought back by Orpheline's soft voice.

"We'll be able to find our way from here. We just need to find the main road."

I nodded although she couldn't see me. "That's good."

She said nothing for a moment, but soon asked the one question I'd been expecting and dreading. "Won't you come with us?"

"No," I said quietly. I heard her sit up.

"Why won't you?"

I sat up, too, but kept my back to her. "I don't belong with you, where you're going. I don't believe in what you're fighting for."

"Not to be too cruel, mate," Sacha said, still lying down, "but you don't really belong with your people anymore, either. You really think they'll want you back on the ship? You just shot the captain."

"Phe shot the captain."

"She sure did. My point's the same, though."

I turned to face the two of them. Sacha had his eyes closed and his arms crossed behind his head. He seemed untroubled.

"How are you so calm?" I asked him. He opened one eye to peer at me.

"I'm just happy to be on land again."

I felt a hand on my shoulder and turned to Orpheline. Her eyes held myriad unnamable emotions, and I found I couldn't look away from her.

"Do you think we could persuade you?" she asked, smiling hopefully. I smiled back, but shook my head all the same.

"No, I don't think so."

"You saved us, though! How can you not care for us but save us like you did?"

I put my hand over hers. "I do care. I care for *you two.* I don't care at all for the rest of your lot. You're just two lucky street rats, is all you are."

"Or very unlucky," she joked, her voice sounding choked. "Had to be stuck with your ugly face for four months." She paused, then asked, "Marin, will you be all right?"

"Sure I will," I told her, trying to sound confident. "I've just got to get back to Paris first. I think I remember enough of your friends' names to keep myself out of too much trouble." I chuckled and looked back in the direction we had come. "Perhaps you two should go."

"Ah, come on Marin," Sacha mumbled. "Let's just sit here for a few minutes, all right?"

So we did. We sat there, and lay there, and simply kept quiet there for more than an hour. Just staring at the light through the trees. I fell asleep at one point and woke up to see the sun beginning to shine through the leaves. I sat up and looked at my sleeping friends.

"Sacha? Phe?" They both opened their eyes immediately and sat up as well. Orpheline stood first, reaching down and pulling the two of us up. We stood awkwardly for a minute, and I thought of all the things I wanted to say to them. Finally, I just said the first thing that came to mind.

"Good luck overthrowing the king, then."

Sacha laughed. "Thank you. All the best stopping us."

He thrust out a hand, and I rolled my eyes, taking it and pulling him in. I wrapped my arms around his middle and squeezed. He stayed still for a moment before sighing and returning the embrace. I held on as long as I could before letting go and awkwardly shoving my hands into my deep pants pockets. He smiled back.

I turned to Orpheline. She was smiling sadly and yet her knees were bent, her posture braced to start running again. I could tell that she was already thinking of the best way to get to their destination.

"Last chance to come along…" she offered.

I smiled and shook my head. "No…maybe next time." She laughed. My brow creased as I looked at her. "Be careful, won't you?" I asked seriously. She nodded and handed me the pistol.

"Take it; I'm sure they'll have guns where we're going." With that she pulled me in quickly, throwing her arms around my neck and squeezing tightly. I held her in return and for a moment the *Tromperie* and Dejafosse and the king and the revolution and the world just disappeared, and it was just the two of us in that peaceful moment.

Then we let go.

She cleared her throat, and I rubbed a hand over my eyes, and we all stared at each other for the last time. I spoke firmly.

"If I ever catch you in Paris again, I'll probably have to turn you in." They nodded, and I nodded, and with one last look at their thin, tired, impossibly determined faces I closed my eyes. "Now go. If you're still here when I open my eyes...I'll shoot you." I felt fingers stroke my cheek lightly then pull away.

It was silent all around me save for the rustle of trees. I counted to a minute and then slowly, so slowly, opened my eyes.

They were gone. On the ground in front of me, wrapped neatly in its string, was the small, brown bandalore.

***

I took my time getting back to the ship. At one point I got turned around and ended up in a small cluster of merchant carts located in a clearing, and I talked for a while to a young woman who was kind enough to give me a cup of water and some yellow fruit for the rest of my walk. I ate it slowly and wandered back into the jungle, too worried that staying on the path—any path—would get me caught. I found the edge where the jungle met the beach just before nightfall and followed the tree line along the sand until finally I neared our ship.

It was just dimming outside, the blue of the sky fading into pinks and reds which glowed and sparkled on the ocean. The men had for the most part finished any outside chores. I knew there would be a handful of men top deck talking, or keeping watch, but for the most part they should all be in the galley, or heading to the sleeping quarters to catch some rest before their turn at watch. As the men cleared the railing I made my way onto the beach. Now that the crew had loaded the goods aboard the Tromperie, there was no more need to stay in India. They would set sail tomorrow.

The sand was warm beneath my feet as I walked through it toward the ship, stopping only when I saw my jacket abandoned on the ground from the night before. I picked it up and put it on, noticing with some small amount of sadness that no longer fit me as it had when I first came aboard. I had grown too much to fit it properly anymore. Slipping the pistol into my dry trousers. Silently as I could, I began to wade into the water on the other side from the dock. Realizing the water was too high, I removed the contents of my pant pockets and tucked them into my shirt, close to my chest. I saw a porthole open ahead of me and began to move toward it. I wanted to climb in and curl up and sleep for the whole journey home.

As I neared it, though, I froze and backed away. I am many things, but a fool I am not, and I would not make the same mistake twice...or the mistake of someone else twice. Instead, I turned away from the porthole and began to make my way toward the back of the ship, where I knew the orlop was.

I reached the tail end of the ship and looked up, counting the portholes from the end of the ship, naming them in my head. *Capstan, unknown, sick bay, orlop, unknown, galley, hold...*I moved sideways until I was below the window between the capstan and the sick bay. Glancing around me once more I flexed my fingers and reached up, digging my nails in between two planks. What would have been impossible in the rain last night was a mere struggle in the warm, dry heat of the early evening, and I slowly worked my way up the ship's wall, my feet finding purchase on the rough wood. I gritted my teeth against the splinters in my fingers until at last I swung my right hand up and grasped the porthole's edge. It was a deep enough sill that I could easily hold onto it, and after peering in to guarantee the room was empty—it was—I pried my nails beneath the glass and pulled, eventually loosening it enough that I could force the window open, cringing as it creaked slightly.

My arms ached and strained as I pulled myself headfirst through the window, slithering through it slowly until I could put my hands out on the floor in front of me and lower myself there. I sighed as my body, dirty and sore and stronger than it had been four months ago, hit the floor. I took a deep breath and opened my eyes, looking around the small space.

It was tinier than the hold, but larger than the closet that Deole had trapped me in a lifetime ago. The air seemed sweet and warm in this room, yet a sour smell reminiscent of a barn wafted from the walls, just as Octave had said it would. There were several bales of hay scattered about and a pile of thick rough cotton cloths, the sort used to pad the goat pens when it was freezing. I moved over to the cloths and draped one over a bale of hay close to the window, laying on it and breathing in and out slowly. I could do this. I could wait it out back to France. I could be a stowaway. Outside the door I heard men laughing and talking, not a one stopping to look inside this room. As for my fate when I got back to Paris? I wasn't too worried about my fate in Paris. I was certain I would be able to work out a deal with whoever meant to lock me up for my crimes.

Sitting up I leaned against the wall, then reached into my shirt. With a small smile, I pulled from it the stolen journal.

By the time Sacha realized my simple embrace was more than just a well-meaning hug, it would be too late for them to risk coming after me.

I hoped they would both be as proud of me as they were furious with me.

I opened the journal and flipped through the pages, feeling my worries ebb with every name I read. I had more than enough here to guarantee me a lifetime of security, should it absolutely come to that. Making my way through the book I came across a familiar page and stopped.

Street Informers:
Sacha Clermont
Orpheline Clermont

I stared at the page for a moment before shaking my head in bemusement at the sheer absurdity of all that had happened. Taking a deep breath I grabbed the page in my hand and tore it from the book, crumpling it in my hands and kneeling on the hay. With one last squeeze of the paper I reopened the window and tossed the page out, watching as it fell into the water, floating until it soaked through; a white speck in a sea of deep blue.

The king would have to win this war with two fewer names.

Sitting back down, I folded my legs underneath me and tilted my head back until it rested against the wall. Soon we would set sail. Soon I would be home. Tomorrow I could figure out the best times to sneak out and steal food, and tomorrow I could decide whether or not to inform Octave of my presence, and tomorrow I could try to learn how to use a bandalore. All of this I could do tomorrow, but for now?

For now I was tired and wanted nothing more than to get a good night's sleep and dream of being back in my house by a fire with a hot meal. With that thought in my mind, I closed my eyes and got as comfortable as I could, preparing myself for a long journey home.

***

Fin